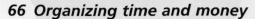

What is the Internet?

The Internet is a vast network of computers linked together, all around the world. It is constantly in the news, and constantly being advertised. You'll hear people talking about e-mail and Web sites, which are an important part of many people's lives, at school, at work or at home.

Over two hundred million people use the Internet worldwide, and millions more are being connected every month. This book will help you to connect to the Internet, and to make the most of your connection.

Why do I need the Internet?

The Internet is a revolutionary way of communicating with people, either one-to-one or with lots of people at once. Whether you want to keep in touch with friends anywhere in the world, find information in seconds about any subject under the sun, get in touch with other people who share your interests, or tell people about yourself or your club, organization or company, the Internet makes it easier for you.

What's on the Internet for me?

The most widely-used Internet facilities are:

E-mail This is a way of sending messages via the Internet to another person or group of people. You can easily recognize an e-mail address because it includes the character @ (at). Find out more about it on pages 18-31.

Mailing lists This is a way for people to share information or opinions about a subject via e-mail. Find out more on pages 32-33.

The World Wide Web This is a huge store of information (including text, pictures, sound and video) which anyone can access from any computer on the Internet. You can recognize an address on the Web because it includes the letters http://www or www. Find out more on pages 34-51.

Chat This is like having a conversation by typing questions and answers. You can "chat" with friends or meet new people, including celebrities. Find out more on pages 74-75.

Newsgroups This is another way for people to share their views, but it is more like public notice boards on the Internet that anyone can read. Find out more on pages 76-79.

Usborne Publishing uses the Internet to tell people about its books.

Web site addresses

In this book you will find the addresses of over 200 Web sites. All of these were correct at the time the book was printed, but Web sites are being created, updated, moved and closed down all the time.

If a Web site has moved, you will generally see a message giving you the new address, and you may be connected to the new address automatically. If a site has closed down, you may have to look for a similar one, perhaps by using a search engine service. You can find out how to use various kinds of search engine on pages 44-49.

THE USBORNE GUIDE TO
THE internet

Mairi Mackinnon and Ben Denne

Designed by Russell Punter and Isaac Quaye
Illustrated by Andy Griffin, Russell Punter and Isaac Quaye

Managing editor: Philippa Wingate

Technical consultants: Liam Devany and Lisa Hughes
With thanks to Rebecca Gilpin and Asha Kalbag

Contents

Don't panic!

If you are new to the Internet, it can seem huge and confusing, full of complicated technical processes and jargon. This book will help you to get started, explaining what equipment (hardware) and programs (software) you need and showing you clearly how to connect to the Internet for the first time.

Once you are connected, or "online", it will help you to find your way around, showing you how to use Internet facilities, such as e-mail, mailing lists and newsgroups, and how to search the Internet for information. It will guide you to a range of interesting Web sites, and even show you how to publish information about yourself by creating your own Web site.

Even if you already use the Internet, you will find lots of tips and useful information in this book to save you time and help you to find what you are looking for.

What equipment do I need?

If you are thinking of buying a computer to connect to the Internet, you will find details of exactly what you need on pages 10-11. This book is mainly intended for people using a PC at home, with Microsoft® Windows® 95 or a later version of Windows as the operating system, and including Microsoft® Internet Explorer. However, the advice and information in the book will be useful to anyone who wants to use the Internet, no matter what equipment they have.

Is it safe to use the Internet?

Nobody actually owns the Internet, but most people and organizations who use it want it to be well-managed and safe. These are some things which worry people:

Offensive material There is a huge amount of good, interesting and useful information on the Internet. There is also information which is upsetting, untrue and even dangerous. You are very unlikely to find this sort of information if you visit Internet sites run by reputable organizations, of which there are a vast number. There are also a number of ways in which you can block offensive material and prevent it from reaching you or your family. You can find out more about filtering material on page 117.

Viruses There are some computer programs, called viruses, which damage your computer, and some of these can be transferred via the Internet. Like viruses in humans, they can be more or less dangerous and you can take steps to avoid catching them – for example, you can get special programs which make your computer more resistant to viruses. You can find out more about viruses and anti-virus software on pages 116-117.

Shopping on the Internet Many people are concerned about buying and selling goods over the Internet, especially when paying by credit card. It is hard to know who you are dealing with when you only contact someone via the Internet, but most reputable Internet companies take great care of your financial details. You can find out more about safe shopping on page 63.

What's on the Internet?

From games to gossip, messages to music, and academic research to shopping, once you have access to the Internet, you can do a huge variety of things. These pages show you just some of them.

Send messages.

Play a wide selection of games.

Research information and fascinating facts.

Communication

There are millions of Internet users all over the world with whom you can communicate, for work or for pleasure. You can send messages, chat, or take part in debates and discussions with other people who share your interests.

Information

There are millions of computers on the Internet storing millions of files of information which are free for you to use. There are dictionaries, maps, timetables, newspapers and magazines, art galleries and cartoons, and information which could help you with your work or hobbies.

Read online newspapers from around the world.

Go on a tour of a museum.

Look at up-to-date weather forecasts.

Find out about films, music and other events in your area.

Tuscany: Take a desktop vacation to the sunny Mediterranean. Feast your eyes on fabulous countryside, sculpture, and grapes on the vine.

Look at pictures and photographs.

Read a selection of cartoons.

Buy music, videos and more.

Enjoy great music and fan clubs.

Look at live pictures from a Web camera.

Search the Internet for a particular word or phrase.

Check timetables and book tickets.

Services

Some computers on the Internet provide you with services. You can use them to get financial advice, find a job, plan a holiday, book tickets for a show and buy anything from airline tickets to videos.

Anywhere, any time

You can connect to the Internet 24 hours a day, seven days a week, anywhere in the world. You can use a computer at home, at school or at work, or a public computer in a library or café. You can even use a portable device, such as a PDA (Personal Digital Assistant, see page 11) or a mobile phone. The Internet can be a part of your everyday life, wherever you are in the world.

Programs

There are lots of programs available for you to copy onto your computer. Some are free to use; others you'll need to pay for. There are programs for playing games, listening to music or watching videos, as well as the latest programs to help you use the Internet more efficiently.

How does the Internet work?

The Internet is a vast computer network linking together millions of smaller networks all over the world.

What is a network?

A network is a group of computers and computer equipment which have been linked together so that they can share information and resources. The computers in an office, for example, are often networked so that they can use the same files and printers.

All the computers linked to the Internet can exchange information with each other. It's as easy to communicate with a computer on the other side of the world as with one that is right next door.

Once your own computer is connected to the Internet, it is like a spider in the middle of a huge web. All the threads of the web can bring you information from other computers.

Servers and clients

There are two main types of computers on the Internet. The ones which store, sort and distribute information are called servers. Those that access and use this information, such as your computer at home, are called clients. A server computer serves a client computer, like a store owner helping a customer.

The picture below shows how the computer networks in different organizations in a town are linked together by the Internet.

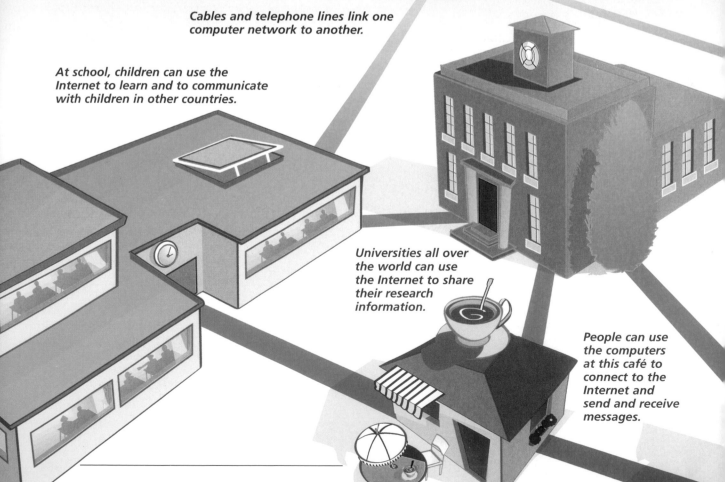

People can connect their computers at home to the Internet.

Cables and telephone lines link one computer network to another.

At school, children can use the Internet to learn and to communicate with children in other countries.

Universities all over the world can use the Internet to share their research information.

People can use the computers at this café to connect to the Internet and send and receive messages.

Telephone lines

The computer networks that make up the Internet are linked together by private and public telephone systems. Computer information is translated into telephone signals and sent from one computer to another in seconds. The cables that link computer networks range from ordinary telephone cables made of copper to fibre optic cables made of thin glass strands. Fibre optic cables can carry huge amounts of information, up to a thousand times faster than copper cable. They are often used for "backbone" connections, which are the most important links between the largest computers on the Internet.

Networks can also be linked by satellite, microwaves, radio waves and infra-red. Networks in different countries and continents are linked by satellites and large undersea fibre optic cables.

This computer belongs to a company that provides people at home or in offices with access to the Internet.

Businesses can use the Internet to exchange information and to sell their products.

Computer talk

To make sure that all the computers on the Internet can communicate with each other, they all use the same language. It is called TCP/IP (Transmission Control Protocol/Internet Protocol), and it ensures that when data is sent from one computer to another, it is transmitted in a particular way and it arrives safely in the right place.

Every computer on the Internet has a unique address, which is actually a long number called an IP (Internet Protocol) number. This enables computers to find each other across the Internet. When you type any Internet address into your computer, your computer converts it into an IP number address in order to send information to the right place.

When one computer sends a piece of information to another computer, the information is broken down into small "packets" of data. Each packet carries the IP number address, specifying where the information has come from and where it is going. The packets travel via the Internet to the destination computer where they are reassembled.

The data that forms this picture is broken into packets.

The packets travel across the Internet.

The picture is reassembled by the destination computer.

What hardware do I need?

Today, many computers are sold as "Internet ready", which means that they have all the hardware and software you need to go online.

However, you don't need a brand new computer to use the Internet. If you have a PC which has at least a 486 processor chip, you will be able to connect to the Internet. If you are using a Macintosh computer, it will need a 68030 processor or better.

Your computer

To use the Internet, your computer will need at least 32 megabytes (MB) of RAM. RAM (Random Access Memory) is the part of your computer's memory which enables it to use programs. Memory is measured in bytes, and 1 megabyte (MB) is just over a million bytes.

Software, and any other information you want to save permanently, is stored on your computer's hard disk. Your computer needs at least 100MB of free hard disk space to store Internet software. (Free space is storage space that isn't being used by other programs.)

Internet connection software (see pages 12-13) is usually supplied on CD, so you will find it easier to get started on the Internet if you have a CD/DVD drive on your computer.

Pictures and sound

You may want to use the Internet to watch video clips, listen to music or play games. All multimedia PCs (PCs designed to play CDs or DVDs) with Pentium processors, and all Macintosh computers, can play video and sound files. If you have an older model, you may need to install some extra hardware.

Video To enjoy the animation and videos that are available on the Internet, your computer needs a powerful graphics card. If your computer doesn't have the right kind of card, the pictures will be fuzzy and will move slowly. You need at least a 32 bit card with 2MB of Video RAM (VRAM).

Sound
If you want to hear sounds on the Internet, such as music clips or voice recordings, your computer must have a sound card and speakers.

Sound cards

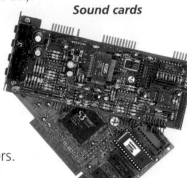

This is a multimedia PC.

CD or DVD drive

This computer has an internal modem.

CPU (Central Processing Unit). The computer's hard drive is stored inside here.

Speaker

Monitor

Keyboard

Mouse

Modems

An external modem

The easiest way to connect to the Internet is by using a device called a modem. This connects your computer to a telephone line and translates computer information into telephone signals and back again. There are three kinds of modems: hardware internal and external modems and software modems. Internal modems fit inside your computer's processing unit, and many new computers have them already installed. An external modem sits on your desk, and has a cable which plugs into one of the sockets in your computer's processing unit. This socket is called a serial port. Hand-held devices, such as PDAs and WAP phones, use software modems in order to make them light and portable.

Modem speed

Modems send and receive information at different speeds. The speed is measured in bits per second (bps). It is best to have the fastest modem you can afford, at least 33,600 bps (33.6Kbps or 33K) and ideally 56,600 bps (56K). If you have a high-speed modem, you will spend less time waiting for pictures or information to appear on the screen. Waiting for information is frustrating, and can be expensive if you are paying for the time you are online.

Your telephone line

You must be able to plug your modem into a telephone point near your computer. If you have only one telephone line, you won't be able to make or receive telephone calls while you are connected to the Internet.

Connecting without a PC

Web TV Using a device called a set-top box, you can browse the World Wide Web and collect e-mail via your television. Web TV offers an easy and inexpensive way to connect to the Internet. However, it is hard to send e-mail or other information yourself without a keyboard and full-power computer.

PDAs and WAP phones These devices can send and receive e-mail or shorter text messages. They can also connect to the World Wide Web, or to special information pages that have been adapted so that they are easier to read on a small screen. You can find out more about them on pages 112-113.

Super-fast connections

For most people connecting to the Internet from home, an ordinary modem is fast enough for their needs. However, speedier connections are available and becoming more popular, although generally they cost more to install and use.

ISDN connection An ISDN line can send and receive data much more efficiently than a modem. It is also much faster, at up to 128Kbps.

Satellite connection This makes it possible to receive information at very high speeds, but you will still need an ordinary telephone modem to send data yourself.

DSL or **ADSL** New technology makes it possible to use your existing telephone line to send and receive data up to ten times faster than a 56K modem.

Internet Service Providers

To connect to the Internet, you will need to sign up with an Internet Service Provider or ISP (sometimes called an Internet Access Provider).

These are some popular ISPs from around the world.

What is an ISP?

An ISP is a company which specializes in connecting people to the Internet. It has a network of server computers across the country or even around the world. You connect to the ISP through your modem and the telephone network, and the ISP connects you to the Internet.

An ISP will provide you with the software you need to go online. It will set up an e-mail address for you, and send and receive your e-mail. It will also have a telephone helpline, or technical support service, which you can call if you have any difficulties in connecting.

For these services some ISPs charge a monthly fee.

How do I choose an ISP?

There are hundreds of ISPs to choose from. Before you decide on one, talk to friends who are already online. Ask them if they would recommend the ISP they use.

You can sign up with an ISP over the phone. You'll find telephone numbers for some of the larger ISPs at the back of this book. Talk to an ISP before you make a decision. In the box below, there are some important questions you should ask them.

Questions to ask an ISP

 Do you have a start-up charge?
Try to avoid paying a charge just to sign up with an ISP, as you will lose the money if you decide to move to another one.

 Is there a monthly fee?
Some ISPs charge a small amount every month for their services.

 Do you charge anything extra for the time I spend online?
Some ISPs offer a number of free hours every month, after which you pay them a small charge for any extra time. Sometimes you can choose to pay a little more in order to have more free hours. Think about how much you expect to use the Internet. If you are likely to use much more than the free time offered, you may be better off with a different ISP.

 Can I connect to the Internet for the cost of a local call?
Most large ISPs use a local call rate number, or even a freecall number, to connect you to the Internet. You certainly shouldn't have to pay more than the cost of a local call for the time you spend online.

 When can I call your helpline, and how much does it cost?
Some ISPs have technical support lines open 24 hours a day, free of charge. With others, you can pay a small annual charge and then call the helpline free of charge as often as you need.

You may have to pay to call other helplines, and they may not be open all day or every day. Make sure the helpline will be available when you need it.

Connection software

An ISP will provide you with all the software you need to get connected to the Internet. Many ISPs give away free CDs with this software; you'll find these CDs in lots of shops and in computer magazines. Other companies will send you the software if you call and ask them for it.

 If you have a Macintosh computer make sure an ISP's helpline offers suitable technical support.

 Is your service suitable for my modem type?
Tell the ISP what kind of modem you have, and your modem speed. You may need to tell them the modem "standard" – you can check this in your modem manual.

 What software do you supply?
If you are using Microsoft® Windows® 95 or a later version of Windows, your ISP should be able to supply its own Internet connection software on CD, ready for you to install. They will probably also include useful extras, such as a Web browser (see page 34) and e-mail software.

If you are using any other operating system, make sure the ISP can provide you with the right software.

 How many e-mail addresses can I have? And how much Web space?
You may not need unlimited e-mail addresses (although some ISPs offer them), but if you are connecting to the Internet at home, it is useful to have different addresses for different members of the family. Many ISPs also offer space for you to build a Web site (you can find out how to do this on pages 80-109).

Online services

Some ISPs, called online services, not only connect you to the Internet, but also offer you a whole selection of news, information and communication services of their own.

Why choose an online service?

Online services are a very popular way of connecting to the Internet as they are easy to use and have many useful features for their members. They have lots of information which is available to their members only. You can keep up with the news and find out about films, music, sport, money matters, travel and hobbies.

You can also "chat" with other members who share your interests. This is like having a conversation, using your keyboard to type questions and answers. As you type, your messages appear on the other members' screens, and they can type their responses.

Sometimes famous people are invited to join organized chat sessions, and you can ask them questions online. If you have friends who use online services, "messenger services" tell you when they are online at the same time as you so that you can chat with them. You can find out more about chat sessions and messenger services on pages 74-75.

These are a few of America Online's information pages and features for its members.

CompuServe has useful information for businesses and professional people.

Which one is best for me?

The best-known online services are America Online (AOL) and CompuServe. You can call their sales departments for free connection software CDs, and they generally offer a free trial period. After that you will pay a small monthly charge for using the service. You can find telephone numbers for AOL and CompuServe at the back of this book.

Different online services suit different people. America Online has a useful feature called "parental controls", for parents who want to protect their children from unpleasant or upsetting material on the Internet. Different levels of parental controls tell AOL to block Internet sites with upsetting content, so that children should not find them even by accident. AOL can act as an excellent guide to the World Wide Web, helping you to find your way around and directing you to interesting sites.

CompuServe is popular with business users, with plenty of up-to-date financial information and good links to business services.

The Microsoft® Network

The Microsoft Network (MSN®) is like an online service, but it is open to everybody who has access to the World Wide Web. You can call for a free connection software CD and use MSN as your ISP, or you can use a different ISP and connect to MSN via the Web.

MSN has home pages for different countries all around the world.

Connecting for the first time

Once you have decided on an ISP or an online service, and received a CD from them, you are ready to install your Internet connection software.

Installing the software

First of all, make sure your computer modem is connected and switched on. Close any programs running on your computer and insert the CD in your computer's CD drive. The installation should start automatically, and instructions will appear on the screen.

You may be asked to restart your computer in order to complete the installation process. You may also be asked to key in a registration number and password; you will find these on the CD cover. If you have any difficulties, you can call the customer support number which you should find on the CD cover.

Choosing a user name

You will then be asked to choose a "user name" or "screen name", and your own password. Your user name will be used as part of your e-mail address, and you can choose any name you like, as long as nobody else has chosen it already. Everyone who uses the same ISP or online service has a different user name, so try to think of a few possible names in case your first choice has been taken by someone else.

You can generally use full stops, hyphens (–) or underscores (_) as part of a user name; you can't use commas, spaces, slashes (/) or brackets. Sometimes you can combine names and numbers; if your name is Anne Jackson, and someone has already chosen anne.jackson, you could be anne.jackson1 or anne.jackson24 (the number could be your birthday).

Max.S?
Max.Surfer?
Max.Surfer_1?

Password tip

Lots of services on the Internet ask you for a password, so try to think of one word which you can use every time. If you think you might forget your password, make a note of it somewhere safe. Some Internet sites require a password which is at least eight letters long. Don't be tempted just to use the word "password"; many sites will not accept it.

When you have finished

Once you have finished installing the software, a message should appear on screen to tell you that the installation was successful.

When you restart your computer, you will see your ISP's icon on your desktop. Double-clicking on this icon will connect you to your ISP, and through your ISP to the Internet.

Virus warning

A virus is a program which damages a computer by destroying information stored on its hard disk. It is possible to pick up a virus over the Internet, and before you connect you should make sure you have anti-virus software installed on your computer. This will work while you are online, and should identify and stop viruses before they can do any damage.

Many new computers have anti-virus software already installed, but you should check that you have the most up-to-date version and update it every few months. New viruses are being invented all the time by people who want to cause damage on the Internet, and the software manufacturers are constantly finding ways of fighting new types of virus. You can find out where to look for anti-virus software on the Internet on page 117.

Making a connection

When you connect to your ISP for the first time, a Dial-up Connection window will appear like the one below, and you will have to type in your password. The first two boxes in the window should have your ISP's name and your user name already filled in. If you fill in your password and then click on the *Save password* box, you will not have to type the password again every time you go online.

Click on the *Connect* button. Your modem will dial the number to connect to your ISP. Below the *Connect* button you may see details of how your connection is progressing. When your modem has made a connection, this window will disappear.

Going online

Once you have a connection, you will be able to open a program called a browser, or it may open automatically. You can find out more about browsers and how to use them on pages 34-39. Inside the browser window will appear your ISP's "home page". This looks a little like the front page of a newspaper.

If you have chosen an online service, the first thing you see when you go online will be a "welcome page". This may have snippets of the day's news, or other information which you might find interesting.

This is the Dial-up Connection window.

Type your password in this space.

Click on this button to connect.

This window shows you what is happening as your modem dials your ISP.

This is the browser window.

This is an ISP's home page.

About e-mail

E-mail, or electronic mail, is one of the most popular facilities on the Internet. You can send a message from your computer to another computer half way around the world, and it could arrive in less than a minute.

E-mail users find ordinary mail so slow that they call it "snail mail". E-mail is also much cheaper than normal mail: you can send a message anywhere in the world for the cost of a local phone call.

How does it work?

Sending e-mail is like sending any other kind of information via the Internet. When you send your message, it is broken down into packets (see page 9) and sent from one computer to another until it reaches its destination.

Do I need special software?

If you have a browser already installed on your computer, or if your ISP has provided you with one, you should find that it includes an e-mail program. Netscape®'s e-mail program, for example, is called Netscape® Messenger. The examples in this book use a program called Microsoft® Outlook® Express, which is part of Microsoft® Internet Explorer. Don't worry if you have a different program – most e-mail programs work in a similar way.

There are several popular free e-mail programs available on the Internet itself, such as Eudora Light and Pegasus (you can find out where to get copies of these on page 123). You can also buy e-mail software; for example, Microsoft® Outlook® is a more advanced version of Outlook Express.

Web-based e-mail

You can use e-mail even if you don't have a direct Internet connection of your own. There are several e-mail services on the World Wide Web, such as Hotmail®, which allow you to send and receive e-mail from any computer anywhere in the world. Find out more about these services on pages 72-73.

E-mail addresses

To send an e-mail, you need to have an e-mail address yourself and you need to know the e-mail address of the person you are sending it to. When you sign up with an ISP, you will be given your own, unique e-mail address, based on your user name (see page 16). All e-mail addresses are made up of the same three elements: a user name, an @ symbol ("at"), and a domain name. Here is a typical address:

mairi@usborne.co.uk
User name "At" Domain name

A user name is usually the person's name or nickname. A domain name might be their ISP's name or the name of the company where they work. The domain name is followed by a few letters which tell you something about the domain – maybe what sort of organization it is, and maybe where it is based.

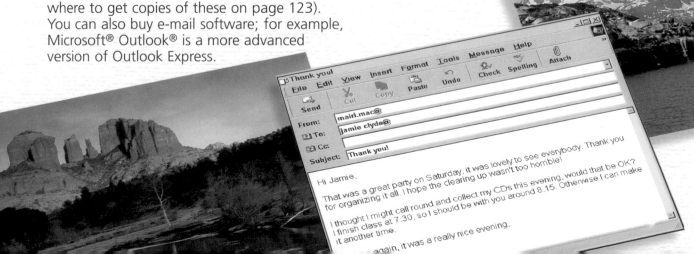

What do the letters mean?

.co or **.com**	a commercial organization
.ac or **.edu**	an educational establishment
.gov	a government organization
.org	an organization, usually not commercial (such as a charity)
.net	an Internet company

There are hundreds of different country codes. Here are just a few of them:

.uk	based in the UK
.ie	based in Ireland
.ca	based in Canada
.au	based in Australia

Domain names in the US don't have a country code, they just end in **.com**, **.edu**, **.org** etc.

How do I find someone's address?

The easiest way to find out someone's address is to ask them. It's best to write the address down, and make sure you have it exactly right – even one missing dot or hyphen will mean your message can't be delivered.

You could also give the person your own e-mail address and ask them to send you an e-mail; their address will appear at the top of their message.

Always keep a record of e-mail addresses, as they can be very difficult to remember exactly.

As well as text messages, you can send e-cards to your friends, like the ones shown here. An e-mail message tells a friend that you have sent them an e-card, and connects them to a Web site where they can see the e-card and a message from you.

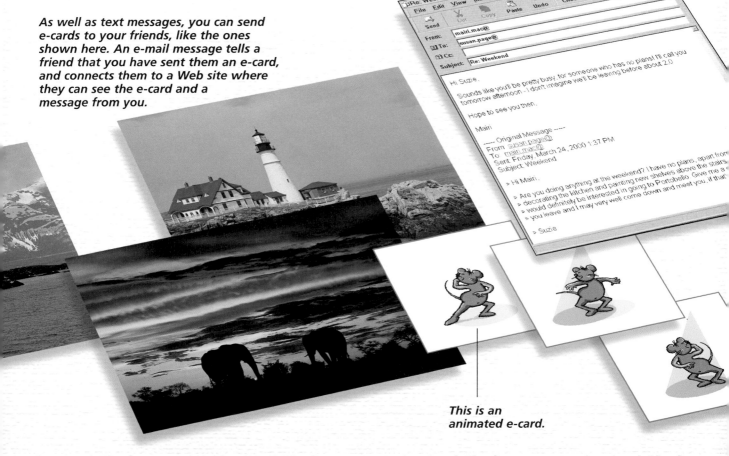

This is an animated e-card.

Sending e-mail

This is the opening window of Outlook Express.

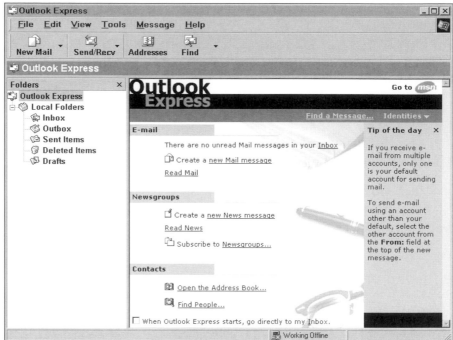

On these pages you will find out how to send an e-mail using Microsoft® Outlook® Express. Even if you have a different e-mail program, you will still find that the steps are very similar.

Getting started

To open your e-mail program, look for the e-mail icon on your desktop and double-click on it. You can also open the program by selecting it in your *Programs* menu (to open this, click on the *Start* button at the bottom left-hand corner of the screen, and then click on *Programs*).

If you are using AOL or CompuServe, go to the Mail Room or Mail Centre. You will find links to these on the Welcome page.

Making a connection

If you connect to the Internet via an ISP, the Dial-up Connection window will appear on top of your e-mail program window – see page 17 to remind yourself what to do next.

If you have already chosen the option *Save password*, all you have to do is click on the *Connect* button, and your modem will dial your ISP and try to connect you. You may hear strange squealing sounds while this is happening. This is your modem working; the sounds will stop once the connection has been made.

If you are sending a long message, or several messages, disconnect from the Internet and write your messages "offline". Otherwise you will have to pay your telephone company for all the time you spend working on your messages before you send them. Even if you do not have to pay for your time online, while your modem is plugged into your telephone line, nobody will be able to call you.

To disconnect from the Internet, look for the the command *Sign Off* (for AOL members), *Access - Disconnect* (for CompuServe) or *Work Offline*. In Outlook Express, *Work Offline* is in the *File* menu.

Sending a message

To make sure that your e-mail is working, try sending a message to yourself.

(1) Click on "Create a <u>new Mail message</u>" or click on the *New Mail* button at the top left-hand corner of the Outlook Express window.

(2) A New Message window will appear.

(3) Click in the *To* box and type in your own e-mail address.

(4) Click in the *Subject* box and type **Test**. This is called the message's "subject line".

(5) Click in the main message area, and type **Test message**.

(6) Click on the *Send* button at the top left-hand corner of the window. If you are working online, the New Message window will close, and you will be able to see the main Outlook Express window again. You may see a **(1)** appear next to the Outbox for a moment. You may also see the message "Sending mail…" at the bottom right-hand corner of the Outlook Express window.

(7) If you are working offline, a window will appear telling you that your message will be stored in the Outbox until you are ready to send it. Click *OK*.

(8) When you are ready to go online, click on the *Send/Recv* button at the top of the window. A window will ask you whether you want to go online. When you click *Yes*, the Dial-Up Connection window will appear.

(9) Another window will appear to tell you that your e-mail program is sending your message. The window will close when your message has been sent.

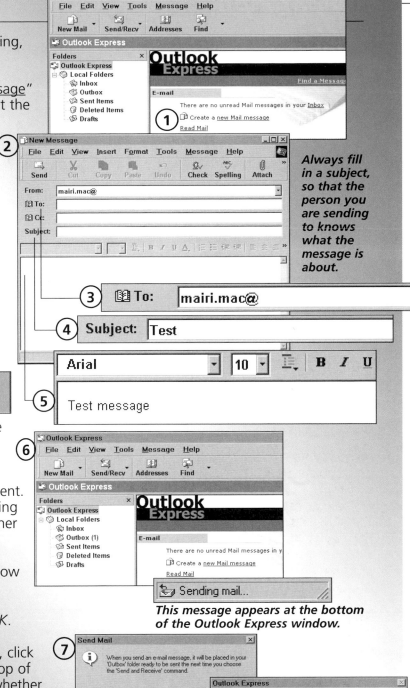

Always fill in a subject, so that the person you are sending to knows what the message is about.

This message appears at the bottom of the Outlook Express window.

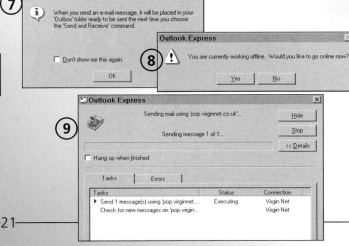

Receiving e-mail

When someone sends you an e-mail, your ISP server stores it in a place called your mailbox. You need to go online to collect e-mail from your mailbox and transfer it to your computer. This is known as downloading your messages.

Reading a new message

If you sent yourself a test message by following the instructions on page 21, you can collect it now.

(1) Open up Outlook® Express. Once your modem has connected, you may see the message "Receiving mail..." at the bottom right-hand corner of the Outlook Express window.

(2) You will see a **(1)** next to the Inbox in your Folders list, and the message "There is <u>1 unread Mail message</u> in your Inbox".

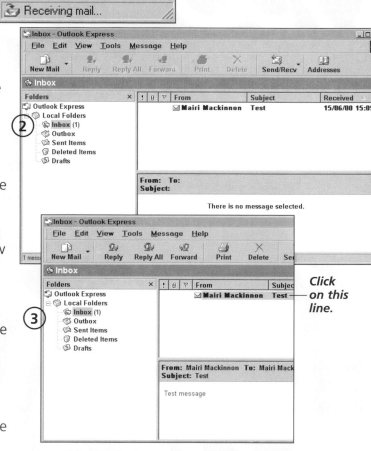

(3) Click on Inbox in the Folders list, or click on this message, and your Inbox window will open. It has two halves. In the top half you will see your message with a closed envelope icon (unread message) which changes to an open envelope icon (read message). In the bottom half you will see the beginning of your message.

Click on this line.

(4) If you double-click on the envelope icon or anywhere on the line beside it showing your name and the Subject line, a message window will open, showing you the message in full. The header (the area above the message window) gives you details of the message – who sent it, its subject and when it was sent.

This part is the message header.

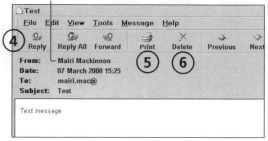

(5) If you want to print out a copy of a message, check that your printer is switched on and ready, then click on the *Print* button in the Toolbar at the top of the screen.

(6) If you don't want to keep the message once you have read it, click on the *Delete* button in the Toolbar.

Replying and forwarding

It's easy to respond to an e-mail. You can send a reply, or send a message on to someone else with your own comments added.

When you receive a message, you will see two or three buttons above or beside the message. Clicking on one of these buttons will open a new message window containing the original message and space for your reply or your comments.

Replying to a message

When you click on the *Reply* button, a new message window appears, addressed to the person who sent the original message. The subject line begins "Re:", followed by the original subject.

The Reply window looks like this.

📖 To:	Nick Bastin
📖 Cc:	
Subject:	Re: Exhibition

```
|———————————————————
----- Original Message -----
From: Nick Bastin
To: Mairi Mackinnon
Sent: Thursday, March 02, 2000 8:50 PM
Subject: Exhibition

> Hi Mairi,
>
> I am so sorry I didn't get your e-mail before as I would have love
> come to the exhibition. I am sorry too that I didn't check my e-ma
> last night, but I got in very late after class.
>
> Are you around at the weekend? Would you like to meet up and
```

Type your answer in this area.

When you start typing, your text appears at the top of the main message window. The original message appears below. You can delete this part if you want, to make your message shorter and easier to read.

Replying to all

If you receive a message that has been sent to a group of people (see "Sending to more than one person", right) you can send a reply to everyone in that group. When you click on the *Reply All* button, a new message window will appear like the Reply window above, but it will be addressed to everybody in the group.

Forwarding a message

To send a message on to another person, click on the *Forward* button. A new message window will appear, like the Reply window, but you will need to fill in the address of the person you are sending the message on to. The subject line begins "Fw:", followed by the original subject.

The Forward window looks like this.

📖 To:	chris@
📖 Cc:	
Subject:	Fw: Concert on Saturday

```
|———————————————————
----- Original Message -----
From: Carola Darwin
To: Mairi Mackinnon
Sent: Tuesday, March 07, 2000 6:44 PM
Subject: Concert on Saturday

> Hi Mairi,
>
> That's great that you can come to the concert. Shall I organize
> and meet you by the main entrance at 7.15?
>
> Would you let Chris know too? I don't have his e-mail address.
```

Fill in the person's e-mail address.

You can type your own comments in this area.

If you want to add anything to the message, start typing and your comments will appear at the top of the main message window, with the original message below.

Sending to more than one person

You can send or forward an e-mail to several different people at the same time. Just type their addresses in the *To* box, separated by ; (a semicolon), like this:

dad@home.net; alex@work.com; kate@work.org

You can also send a copy of the e-mail to one or more people, to let them know what you have said. Type their addresses in the *Cc* box, separated by a semicolon if you are sending copies to more than one address.

Writing good messages

"Hello", no, er.."Hi"... "Hiya"..?

When you first send e-mail, you may feel awkward and your messages may be rather stiff and formal. When you are used to sending e-mail, on the other hand, it's easy to be careless and even say things you don't really mean. This section will help you to write messages which are clear and easy to read.

Tips for good messages

@ Always give your message a subject, saying briefly and clearly what the message is about. For example, "Any plans for Saturday night?" is much clearer than just "Saturday", and easier to read than "I wondered if you were doing anything on Saturday night."

@ Keep your messages fairly short and simple. It is tiring to read a long message on a computer screen.

@ If your message is fairly long, use short paragraphs and spaces in between paragraphs, to make it easier to read.

@ When you are replying to a message, or forwarding one, don't include all of the original message. Delete the parts which aren't important (find out how to do this on the next page).

@ Don't use bold or italic letters, as different e-mail programs from yours may not show them when they display a message. You can emphasize a word or words by putting *asterisks around them*, like this.

@ Check your spelling. It's easy to write a message in a hurry and then send it before you notice silly mistakes. Read through the message carefully on the screen before you send it; you might like to use the spelling checker if your e-mail program has one. In Outlook® Express, the spelling checker is in the *Options* menu (see page 26).

Hope you are feling betta.

@ Don't send messages in capital letters. This is the e-mail equivalent of SHOUTING!

@ Don't reply to a message in too much of a hurry. When you answer a letter, you have a little more time to think about your answer before you post it, but it's easy to send a hasty reply to an e-mail and then regret it. Sending angry or rude e-mail is called "flaming".

@ Be careful if you are including funny comments. When you are speaking to somebody face to face or on the telephone, it is easy for them to tell if you are joking, but people can mistake the tone of an e-mail. If you think you might be misunderstood, you can always add a "smiley" (see page 33).

@ Be careful what you write. E-mail is not always private, and messages can accidentally be sent to the wrong person.

@ It's polite to reply to e-mails as soon as you can. With a letter, you could leave your reply for a few days, but with e-mail people may expect a reply within a day. If you know you can't answer right away, you can always send a brief message to let the other person know you have received their message and will answer properly as soon as you are able to.

Editing a message

When you are replying to a message, or forwarding one (see page 23), the original message will appear in the new message window. Normally your answer will appear above the original message.

You can delete part or all of the original message. You should definitely do this when you are replying to a reply (or even a reply to a reply), otherwise every message in the sequence appears every time, and the messages become impossibly long.

Select the part you want to delete. Highlight it by clicking at the beginning and dragging your mouse cursor to the end of the text you want to delete. Then press the *Delete* key on your keyboard.

You can also quote sections of text by highlighting them in this way and using the *Edit – Copy* and *Paste* commands in the menu bar.

Your answer will appear here, at the top.

Earlier messages may appear inside arrow signs, like this.

You may want to delete this, your original message.

After editing, your reply might look like this.

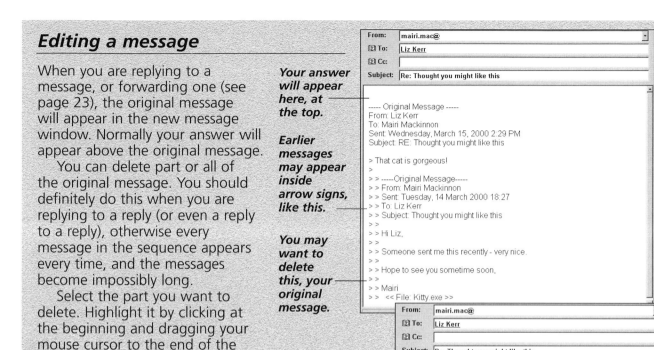

Replying to specific points

You can choose to answer the points made in a message one by one. To do this, edit the message as much as you need to, as described above. Then place your cursor after the point you are replying to, press the Return key and type your answer. Leave one line space before and after your replies.

Some e-mail programs use arrows before each line in the original message. The person you are replying to can see which lines are your replies, as they don't have any arrows. Some e-mail programs use indents – starting the line a little further to the right – instead of arrows. Others show the text of replies in a different colour, although the colour may not come out in a different e-mail program, so it's best always to leave space before and after your replies to make them clear.

This is part of the original message.

This is part of the reply.

This reply answers points one by one.

Personalizing your e-mail program

Once you know how to send and receive messages, there are several ways in which you can personalize your e-mail program.

You can change the look of your messages and add a personal signature. You can also create an address book for e-mail addresses you use often.

A shortcut to your Inbox

You can set up Microsoft® Outlook® Express so that when you open the program, you see your Inbox and any new messages in it right away.

When you open Outlook Express, you will see an option at the bottom of the screen: "When Outlook Express starts, go directly to my Inbox". Click on the box beside this option.

Click here. ──────

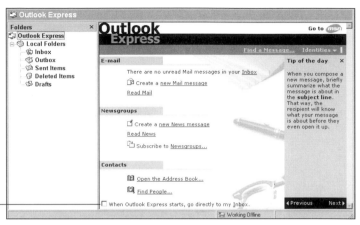

Choose options from these headings.

Click here to add the signature to all your messages.

Type your signature text here.

Click OK. ──

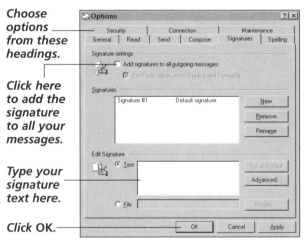

Outlook Express options

Most of the commands for personalizing Outlook Express are in the Options window. To open this window, click on *Tools* on the menu bar, and then *Options...* A window will appear like the one on the left.

Click on any of the headings across the top of the window to bring up a different set of options. You can change the settings for sending and receiving mail, checking spelling before you send a message or adding your own signature.

This is the Options window for creating a personal signature.

E-mail signatures

An e-mail signature could include your name, nickname or slogan, a joke or a quotation. If you use e-mail at work, you might want to give your department name or your job title. Otherwise it's best not to include personal information such as your home address.

E-mail signatures can also include pictures made up of keystrokes. If you try this, keep the picture fairly simple as it may not look quite the same in a different e-mail program.

These are examples of e-mail signatures.

The picture on the right is made up of keystrokes.

```
                \\|||||///7
                 \\||||/||//
                / ~ | ~ |    nnn
              --\  0 |0 /   nl|||
               \ ?  _\ \    || |
               U\  \_/ /    \_/
                \__/        &&&
              &&&/__ /&&&&  &&&
              &&&&&&&&&&&&&&
              &&&&&&&&&&&&&&
              &&&&&&&&&&&&&
```

```
***********************************
"Nìl sa saol seo ach ceo is nì bheimìd beo
ach seal beag gearr."
("It's a misty old world, and we are only in
it for a short, sharp while") - Irish proverb.
***********************************
```

Creating an address book

You don't need to type in someone's e-mail
address every time you send them an e-mail.
You can save addresses in an address book,
and select one when you start a new message.

(1) Click on the *Addresses* button in the
Toolbar.

(2) An Address Book window will open.
Click on the *New* button and select
New Contact...

(3) A Properties window will open. You can
enter as many details as you like about the
person by clicking on the keywords across the
top of the window, but you should at least
enter their name and e-mail address.

(4) When you have entered the details, click
OK. The Properties window will close and
you will see your new contact listed in your
address book.

(5) Close the Address Book. If you want to
send an e-mail to someone in the book,
click on the *New Mail* button in the Toolbar.
A New Message window will open.

(6) Click on the Address Book symbol next to
the *To* button. A Select Recipients window
will appear with a list of your contacts. Click on
the name of the person you are writing to, and
then click on the *To* button to the right of the
list. Your contacts name will appear in the box
beside the *To* button.

(7) Click *OK*. The Select Recipients window will
close, and your contact's name will appear in
the *To* box of your message header.

You can choose to have e-mail addresses added
to your address book automatically when you
reply to an e-mail. To do this, click on *Tools* in the
menu bar, then select *Options...*
and then *Send*. You will see the
option *Automatically put people
I reply to in my Address Book*.
Make sure there is a tick in the
box beside this option.

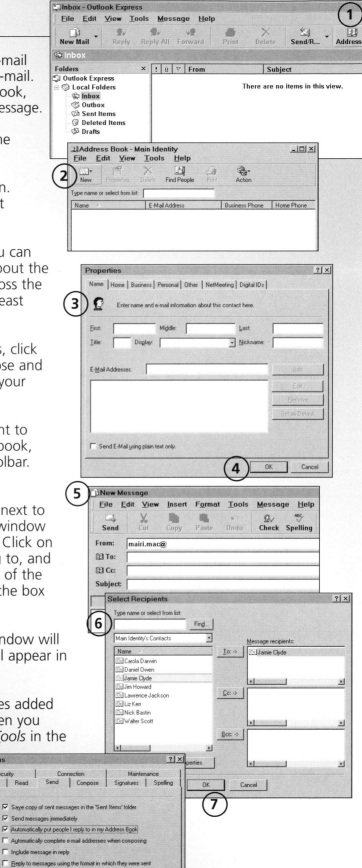

Organizing your e-mail

When you start sending and receiving lots of messages, you will find your Inbox and your Sent Items folders soon fill up with old messages. You may want to keep some of these; others you may want to delete permanently. These pages show you how to organize your messages, making your e-mail program much easier to use.

Deleting messages

To delete a message in any of your folders, click on it to select it. Then click on the *Delete* button at the top of the screen.

Your message will be sent to the Deleted Items folder, but it will not be deleted permanently. If you decide that you still need it after all, click on the Deleted Items folder. Click on the message and hold your mouse button down as you drag your message back into the Inbox. Your mouse cursor will change to a ⊘ symbol, which becomes an arrow again once it is over your Inbox. Release the button, and the message will be left in your Inbox.

You can also move a message by selecting it, clicking on *Edit* in the menu at the top of the screen, and then clicking on *Move to Folder...* This will open a "Move" window, and you can choose the folder where you want to store the message.

Deleting messages permanently

From time to time, you will need to empty your Deleted Items folder. To do this, click on the folder and select all the messages by clicking on the first message, holding down the Shift key and clicking on the last message in the list. Then click on the *Delete* button. A message will appear asking whether you are sure you want to delete the messages. Click on *Yes* and the messages will be deleted.

Click on Yes to delete messages.

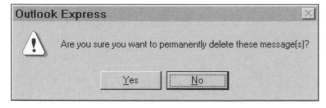

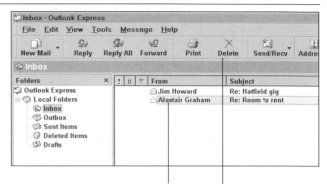

This message is selected.　　**Delete *button***

If you receive an e-mail from an address you don't recognize, the safest thing is to delete it without opening it.

Some e-mail, called "spam", is like the junk mail sent through the postal system. It is used to advertise products you probably don't want, and just clutters up your Inbox. When you give your e-mail address, for example when you are filling in a company form, look for a box you can tick if you don't want to receive advertising e-mail from the company.

Occasionally e-mail can contain viruses, usually as attachments to the e-mail (see page 31). Always make sure you have up-to-date anti-virus software.

More often, you will receive warnings of e-mail viruses, asking you to pass the warning on to everyone you know. Don't panic! These messages are hoaxes. They are always undated, and can circulate for years. Just delete the message.

Storing messages in folders

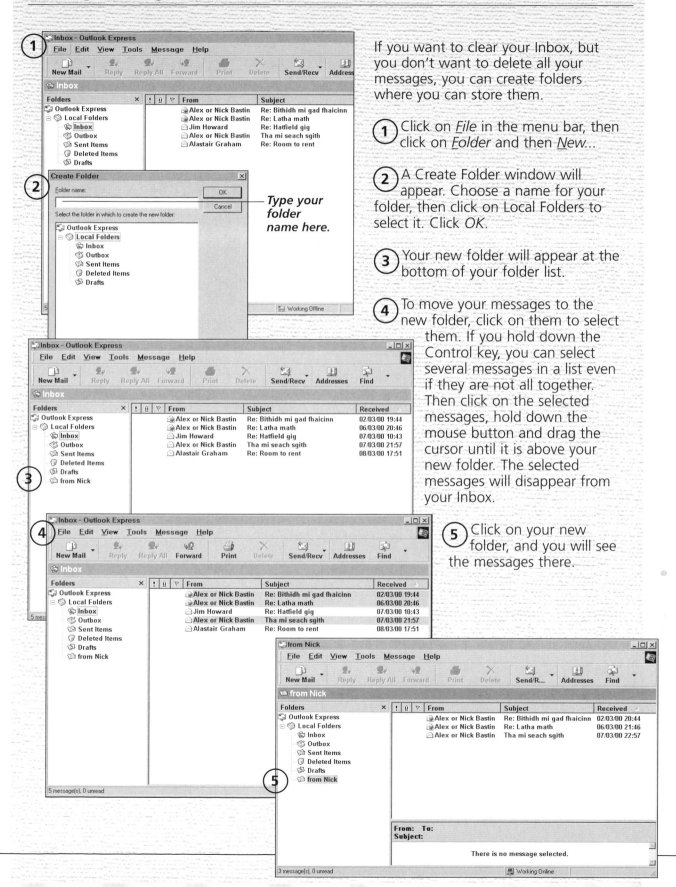

If you want to clear your Inbox, but you don't want to delete all your messages, you can create folders where you can store them.

1 Click on *File* in the menu bar, then click on *Folder* and then *New...*

2 A Create Folder window will appear. Choose a name for your folder, then click on Local Folders to select it. Click *OK*.

3 Your new folder will appear at the bottom of your folder list.

4 To move your messages to the new folder, click on them to select them. If you hold down the Control key, you can select several messages in a list even if they are not all together. Then click on the selected messages, hold down the mouse button and drag the cursor until it is above your new folder. The selected messages will disappear from your Inbox.

5 Click on your new folder, and you will see the messages there.

Type your folder name here.

Attachments

You can send many different kinds of files with an e-mail message, by "attaching" them to the message. You can attach files you have created in other programs, such as word-processing or spreadsheet files, so that someone else can look at your work. You can also send pictures, music and even video clips, as long as they are in a form which can be stored on your computer.

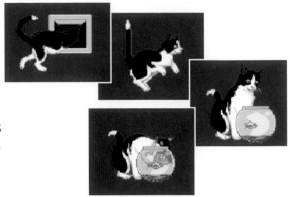

This is an "exe", or executable file. Exe files are programs in themselves. This one will run an animated figure of Felix the cat, which plays on your desktop.

Attaching a file

To attach a file in Outlook® Express, follow the instructions below. Most other e-mail programs work in a similar way.

(1) Open a New Message window and fill in the header as you would normally. Write any message you want to send with the attachment.

(2) Click on the *Attach* button above the message window, or click on *Insert* in the Menu bar and select *File Attachment...*

(3) An Insert Attachment window will appear. Choose the file you want to insert, and click on it to select it, then click on *Attach*.

(4) A new line will appear in your message header, with details of your attachment.

(5) Click on the *Send* button. Your message and its attachment will be sent as normal.

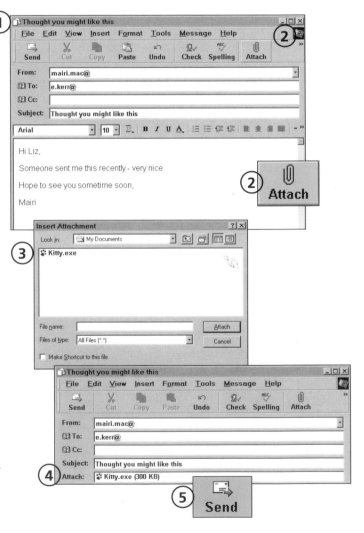

Opening an attachment

When you receive an e-mail with a file attached, it will appear in your Inbox like a normal message, but you will also see a paperclip symbol to the left of the envelope icon.

(1) Double-click on the message to open it as you would normally.

(2) You will see the attachment in a line below the Subject line. Double-click on the name of the attachment to open it.

(3) You will see an Open Attachment Warning window. If you want to open the attachment right away, click on *Open it* and then click *OK*.

(4) If you want to save the attachment and look at it later, click on *Save it to disk*. A Save Attachment As window will appear, and you can choose where you want to keep the attachment on your computer.

Remember, it's best not to open e-mails or attachments from a person you don't know, as they could contain viruses (see page 28).

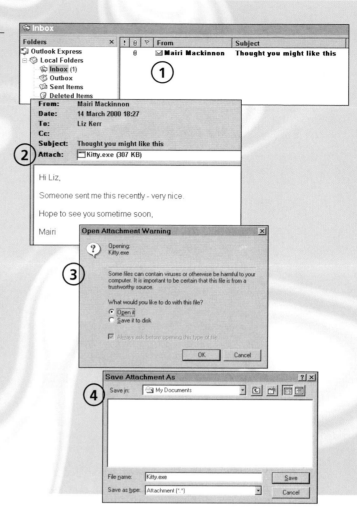

Large files

If you are sending an attachment with an e-mail, make sure that it is not too big to send. Files over 1MB in size can cause problems.

If you connect to the Internet using an ordinary modem, a large file can take time to send or receive. Some ISPs will not accept large attachments, so if you do have to send a large file, make sure that both your ISP and the ISP of the person you are sending to will accept it.

You may be able to break the file up into several smaller files. Alternatively, you could compress it using a program such as WinZip® (for PCs) or StuffIt™ (for Macintosh computers). You can get copies of these via the Internet (see page 43). If you send a compressed file, make sure that the person you are sending it to has the same program, so that they can decompress the file when they receive it.

Can I send an attachment to anyone?

Not everyone can receive attachments. Some business networks reject all exe files as a matter of course, in case they contain viruses. Exe files created on a PC will generally not work on a Macintosh computer, and vice versa.

Some other files, such as graphics, sound or video files, can only be opened if you have the right software. For video files, this might be RealPlayer® or QuickTime™, both of which are available on the World Wide Web (see page 41).

Mailing lists

You can use e-mail to get in touch with people all over the world who share your interests, simply by joining a mailing list. There are hundreds of thousands of mailing lists covering every subject you could imagine. You can even set up a list of your own.

How do mailing lists work?

There are two main types of mailing list: announcement lists and chat lists.

Announcement lists are usually run by organizations and are used to send out information. For example, a rock band might use an announcement list to publicize their tours and recordings.

Chat lists are more like newsgroups (see pages 76-79) except that you communicate with the other people on the list by e-mail. You send an e-mail to the mailing list itself, and it is then forwarded to all the other people on the list. Many sports teams have mailing lists for fans to discuss recent games.

How do I find out about a list?

The best place to find out about mailing lists is the World Wide Web (find out how to use the Web on pages 34-39).

Two Web sites which have information about mailing lists are **www.liszt.com** and **paml.alastra.com** (PAML stands for Publicly Accessible Mailing Lists). Liszt sorts mailing lists into subject categories to help you find lists which match your interests.

For example, if you are looking for lists about world music, you would click on *Music* to see a full list of music categories, and then on *World* to see a selection of world music mailing lists.

This is Liszt's Web site.

Type the subject you are looking for in this box.

Both Liszt and PAML have Search options, where you type in a word (or a few words, for a more precise search) and the search will find related lists for you. For example, if you are looking for mailing lists about basketball, type **Basketball** in the Search box and you will get a selection of lists for coaches, fans and players. If you type **Basketball fans** (**Basketball;fans** on PAML's site) you will get lists for fans only.

How do I join a list?

Joining a mailing list is called subscribing. To subscribe to a list, you send an e-mail to the list itself or to the list moderator (the person who manages the list). If you find out about a list through the Liszt or PAML Web sites, the Web site will tell you who you should address your first e-mail to, and what you should put in your message.

Once you have subscribed to a list, you will receive a welcome message telling you more about the list. Keep a copy of this message, as it will tell you how to leave the list, or unsubscribe, if you want to.

Setting up your own list

If you can't find a mailing list for a particular subject, or if you want to keep in touch with a particular group of friends, you may like to set up your own list. A mailing list can be a great way to stay in touch with a year group at school or college, for example.

There are several Web sites which will set up and administrate a list for you, free of charge. You can choose whether to make your list public or private: a public list will be included in directories, and anyone can choose to join it.

One site which will set up a mailing list for you is **www.egroups.com**. The site gives you full, clear instructions on how to start up a list and then how to run it.

Tips for using mailing lists

@ Only subscribe to one or two lists at first, otherwise you may receive more e-mail than you can manage.

@ If you have joined a chat list, wait a little while before you send any messages yourself. Read the messages sent to the list for a week, and you will see how the other members communicate and avoid repeating points that have been made recently.

@ When you reply to a message, include the point you are responding to in the original message. This is called quoting. You can find out how to quote part of a message on page 25.

@ If a list sends out lots of messages every day, you might ask to be sent a summary of messages once a day or once a week, so that you are not constantly receiving e-mail. This summary is called a digest.

@ Unsubscribe from a list when you are going away, and subscribe again when you get home. Otherwise you may find hundreds of messages waiting for you.

Smileys and shorthand

In an e-mail, it's sometimes hard to tell whether a person is being serious or making a joke. If you want to show that you are joking, you can use a "smiley" or "emoticon" made up of characters on your keyboard. When you look at a smiley sideways, it looks like a face.

There are hundreds of different smileys. Here are a few of them:

 :-) Smiling   0:-) Angel

 ;-) Winking   :-o Surprised

 :-D Laughing   <:-) Dumb question

 :-(Sad face   :-P Sticking tongue out

 :/) Not funny   :*) Clowning around

It's best not to use too many smileys when you are sending a message to a mailing list for the first time, however, as not everyone appreciates them.

To save time typing, some e-mail users have developed acronyms which are abbreviations of often-used phrases. Here are some you might see:

AFAIK   As Far As I Know

BTW   By The Way

FYI   For Your Information

IMHO   In My Humble Opinion

LOL   Laughing Out Loud

ROFL   Rolling On the Floor Laughing

NRN   No Reply Necessary

TIA   Thanks In Advance

The World Wide Web

The World Wide Web, sometimes just called the Web, is probably the most exciting part of the Internet. It is used by organizations and individuals to publish all kinds of information. Millions of people have access to this information, and most of it is free. The Web is huge, and growing all the time.

What can I use it for?

You can use the Web to get news from around the world, events listings, pictures, music and movie previews. You can buy – and sell – anything and everything, from houses to holidays. You can look for detailed information about a particular subject, or you can explore and find things which catch your interest.

What is a Web site?

When you see an address beginning www, or http://www, you know that it is the address of a Web site. Web site addresses are called URLs (Uniform Resource Locators).

Information on the Web is displayed on "pages", like those shown below. A Web site may have one or more pages. Most companies have Web sites, where you can find information about the company and perhaps buy their products. Newspapers and magazines publish online versions on their Web sites. Some companies only operate via the Web, offering information, goods or services.

You can find online newspapers, banks and travel agencies, museums and art galleries, book and music stores on the Web.

People can also create their own Web sites, to tell other people about themselves or their interests. Sometimes "unofficial" Web sites, created by fans, are just as interesting and attractive as "official" sites. Find out how to create your own Web site on pages 80-109.

How do I get on to the Web?

If you connect to the Internet via an online service, you can get on to the Web simply by typing a URL into the Keyword (or Go word) box at the top of the screen. Otherwise you will need a program called a browser.

The two most widely-used browsers are Microsoft® Internet Explorer and Netscape® Navigator, which is included in the Netscape Communicator package. You may have one or other of these already installed on your computer, or your ISP may have provided you with a copy. Look for a browser icon on your computer desktop, and double-click on this icon to open your browser.

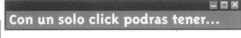

The home page

The first page you will see is your browser's home page – or your ISP's home page, if your browser was supplied by your ISP. This looks a little like the front page of a newspaper. You can start exploring the Web from the home page itself, by clicking on pictures or highlighted text.

Web pages and Web sites are connected by a vast network of links called hyperlinks. These take you from one page to another, related page. There are two ways of seeing whether an item

is a hyperlink: if it is in a piece of text, the link itself will usually be in a different colour from the rest of the text and may also be underlined. A picture can also be a hyperlink. With both text and picture links, your mouse cursor will change from an arrow to a pointing hand when it is on top of a link.

Clicking on the link will take you to the linked page, which will start to appear in your browser window in place of the page you were looking at previously.

The main page shown below is an ISP's home page. The arrows show how text and picture links connect to different pages.

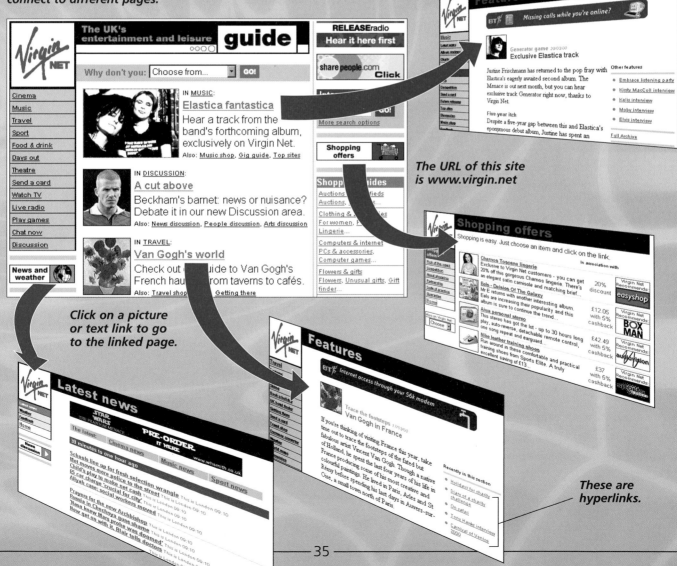

Click on a picture or text link to go to the linked page.

The URL of this site is www.virgin.net

These are hyperlinks.

Exploring the Web

The Web can be a confusing place, until you know how to get around it. Your browser will help you to explore the Web without getting lost.

Check out a Web site

You can go to any Web site by typing its URL in the Address box (or Netsite box, in Netscape® Navigator) at the top of your browser's window. To get used to using your browser, you could try exploring the NASA Web site. Type the URL **www.nasa.gov** in the Address box, and press the Return key.

This is a browser's toolbar.   *Type the URL here.*

The NASA home page will start to appear in your browser's window, in place of your browser's or ISP's home page. The page builds up gradually as pictures and text are copied from the NASA server computer to your computer's memory. This process is called downloading. Most Web pages don't take very long to download, but pages with a lot of pictures or animation may take a few minutes.

This is NASA's home page.

Follow the links

You can use the links on this page to find pictures taken by the Galileo space probe. First, scroll down the page by using your mouse to drag the slider bar on the right-hand side, until you get to the section "Cool NASA Websites", towards the bottom of the page.

*You will find links like this
further down NASA's home page.*   *Slider bar*

Now click on the picture "Galileo". The Galileo project home page will start to download.

The Galileo project home page

Click on "Images from Galileo" and you will be able to look at a range of pictures of the probe, as well as photographs transmitted back to Earth by the probe itself. If you click on any of the pictures, you will download a new page with information about the picture and links to others like it.

The Back and Forward buttons

When you have finished looking at a picture, you may want to go back to the previous page in order to look up others. You can do this easily by using the *Back* button on your browser, in the top left-hand corner of your browser window. Click on the *Back* button, and the previous page will appear, much more quickly than it did when you first downloaded it. This is because your computer stores a copy of all the pages you download in a browsing session.

Similarly, if you have gone back a page but you decide you would like to see the other page again, you can use the *Forward* button.

The Stop and Refresh buttons

Sometimes you may decide that you do not want to look at a page after all, or you think it is taking too long to download – it may have a lot of picture files, or there may be a problem with the server for that Web site. If you decide that you do not want to wait any longer, click on the *Stop* button. The page will stop downloading, and you can go back to the previous page or type in a different URL.

If you think the page you are looking at is not the most complete or up-to-date version – it may be a version you downloaded at the beginning of a browsing session, or it may not have downloaded all its picture files – you can click on the *Refresh* button to tell your browser to download a new copy of the page.

The Home button

Click on the *Home* button to go back to your browser's (or your ISP's) home page.

You can choose to have a different Web site as your home page, if you like. Find out how to do this on page 51.

Find out how to do this on page 51.

Sites worth seeing

Try browsing the following sites:

www.whitehouse.gov

www.bbc.co.uk

www.tate.org.uk

These organizations have Web sites you might like to explore.

Type carefully

You must type a URL correctly in order to connect to the right Web site. Be careful with the abbreviations at the end of a domain name – is it ".com" or ".net", ".gov" or ".org"?

If you mis-type a URL you may be connected to a different Web page altogether. More often, you will get an error message like the one below. Check the URL, if you have a record of it, and try typing it again.

> **The page cannot be displayed**
>
> The page you are looking for is currently unavailable. The Web site might be experiencing technical difficulties, or you may need to adjust your browser settings.

This message may mean you have typed the URL incorrectly.

Save it for later

You will soon find that there are Web pages you want to go back to again and again. There are several ways of storing Web pages or URLs so that you can find them quickly.

The History button

The History panel shows you the names and URLs of sites you have visited in the past two weeks.

Internet Explorer keeps a record of all the Web sites you have visited recently, so if you remember visiting a site but you don't have its URL, you can check your History. Click on the *History* button and a panel, like the one shown on the right, will open on the left-hand side of your browser window.

"Favorites"

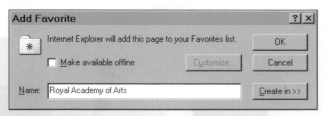

You can instruct your browser to keep a record of sites you want to look at again. Internet Explorer calls these Favorites (in Netscape, they are called Bookmarks).

When you find an interesting site, click on *Favorites* in the menu bar at the top of your browser window, and then on *Add to Favorites...* You will see a message like the one below. Check the name given to the site – you can change it if you want – and click *OK*.

*Use the **Add to Favorites...** command to keep a record of a site so that you can find it again easily.*

When you want to visit a site in your list of Favorites, just click on the *Favorites* button and then click on the name of the site in the panel.

Organizing your Favorites

In time, you will have a long list of sites. You can use the *Organize...* button at the top of the Favorites panel to sort these into folders, or to delete sites you no longer want. When you click on a site name, you will see its details in the box to the left, including how often you have visited it in the past two weeks.

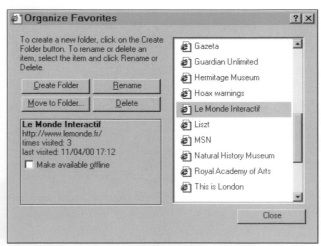

This window shows you details of a site in your Favorites list.

Saving pictures

You might want to save a copy of a picture you find on a Web site. To do this, click on the picture with the right-hand button on your mouse and a menu will appear. Click on *Save Picture As...* and a window will open like the one below.

Use the *Save in:* box to select the folder where you want to save the picture. Use the *File name:* box to choose a name for it and then click on the *Save* button.

Use this window to choose where you want to save a picture, and to give it a file name.

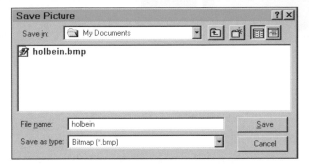

You can then find the picture file in the folder you have selected. Double-click on the file to open it.

Copyright

Most of the information on the Web is available free. This doesn't mean that you can do what you like with it. Information and pictures generally belong to the person who created them, or to an organization representing that person. This is called "intellectual property" or "copyright".

You can save information onto your computer for your personal use, but if you want to publish either pictures or text in any way (including elsewhere on the Web), you must get permission from the person or company that owns the copyright. If you don't do this, you may be breaking the law.

These pictures are from the Web site of the Louvre museum in Paris at www.louvre.fr

Saving text

The easiest way to save text from a Web site is to select it with your mouse cursor and copy it into a new file, such as a word processing document. To do this, highlight the text you want to copy and then click on *Edit* in the menu at the top of your browser window, and then *Copy*. Open your new document and click on *Edit* and then *Paste* to insert the text.

Working offline

You need to be online to download new pages, but if you want to go back through the pages you have downloaded in a browsing session and look at them in more detail, it's better to work offline. This will save you money on your phone bill, or time if your ISP allows you only a certain amount of connection time free of charge.

Click on *File* in the Menu bar at the top of your browser window, and then click on *Offline* or *Work Offline*. You will see a message asking whether you want to hang up the modem. Click on *Yes*.

To check that you are offline, look for a symbol like one of these at the bottom of your browser window.

These buttons show that you are offline.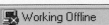

Plug-ins

Some Web sites include features, such as sound or animation, which you will only be able to see or hear if you have a particular kind of software installed on your computer. The software is called a "plug-in", and works with your browser to give it extra features.

Where can I find the software?

Sometimes you can find direct links to plug-ins from a Web site. For example, you might click on the link to a video clip. If you do not have the right plug-in on your computer, you may see a link to the site where you can download it. Click on the link, and follow the instructions you are given. Otherwise you can download plug-ins from the Web sites listed on the page opposite.

If you are asked where on your computer you want to install a plug-in, select the Plug-ins folder in your browser folder, which you will find in your Program Files folder.

Are plug-ins safe?

If you download any software over the Internet, there is a small risk that you could download a virus or some other element in the software which could damage your computer. Usually you will get a warning message like the one shown below.

Click on Yes if you are sure you want to continue with the installation.

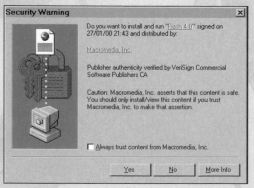

Can I manage without the plug-in?

Different plug-ins work in different ways. Some, such as QuickTime™ or RealPlayer® (see opposite), are only used for one part of a site, such as a sound or video clip. If you don't have the plug-in, you will not be able to watch or listen to the clip, but you will be able to explore the rest of the site.

Other plug-ins, such as Flash™ animation (see opposite), are an important part of the whole site's design. You may have the choice of looking at a non-Flash version of the site, but otherwise you will not be able to see most of the site's contents.

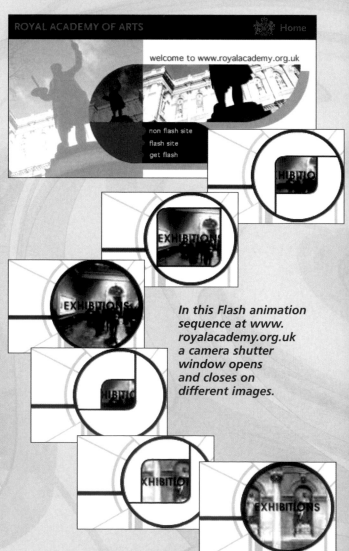

In this Flash animation sequence at www. royalacademy.org.uk a camera shutter window opens and closes on different images.

Java™

One of the most widely-used animation effects is Java. Java is American slang for coffee, and just as coffee makes people more animated, Java can be used to make Web pages look more lively. It is actually not so much a plug-in as a programming language which creates small programs called applets. These might be moving text or small animated figures which can then be inserted in Web pages.

Java is designed to be recognized by all browsers, but early versions of Netscape® and Internet Explorer may not recognize applets. If you have problems with Web pages containing applets, try downloading a more up-to-date version of your browser (for more information on downloading see pages 42-43).

RealPlayer®

If you want to listen to music on the Internet, you will need a plug-in. Most online music stores and radio stations use a process called RealAudio® to put music clips on their Web sites, and to play RealAudio clips you will need RealPlayer. RealPlayer also includes RealVideo®, which is used by television network sites for video clips, and also for movie previews and Webcasts (see page 59).

Other popular plug-ins for listening to music online include MP3 players. You can find out more about MP3 on page 59.

QuickTime™

QuickTime is another plug-in which is used to play video clips. It also includes QTVR (QuickTime Virtual Reality), which can be used to show 360° views, for example on a tour of a building. You can click on an image and move it around or zoom in and out, as though you were controlling a video camera. Find out more about virtual reality on pages 70-71.

Shockwave® for Flash™

Flash animation is used to create fast-moving text and images which can make sites look spectacular. Flash sites generally download and run quickly and smoothly, and the images are clearer than other kinds of animation. Many official band sites, as well as official sites of the latest films, use Flash.

Watch as the camera pans around the harbour and night turns to day at www.mycity.com.br/ mycitysites/barcelona

Shockwave® for Director®

Shockwave for Director is used to create interactive sites, which are especially good for games. On an interactive site you make things happen by moving or clicking your mouse – you can make characters move, or turn objects around, or explore a virtual area, or choose and play sound or video clips. Shockwave allows you to look at sites containing animation, video and sound, which can all be played together in one file.

These figures are part of a game at www.mycity.com.br/mycitysites/london

Plug-in sites

RealPlayer® : **www.real.com**

QuickTime™ : **www.apple.com/quicktime**

Shockwave® : **www.macromedia.com/ shockwave/download**

Downloading programs

You can find lots of sites on the Web offering software for you to download, or copy on to your computer. Software downloads might include programs to help you use the Internet more efficiently, programs to help you at work and games programs. Many of these are available free of charge.

Looking for software

A good place to start looking for software on the Internet is your browser's or your software manufacturer's home page. You might find useful plug-ins (see page 40), or an updated version of your browser.

There are also a number of sites which have lists of links to downloads, news and reviews of new programs. Some of these are listed in the box on the page opposite.

Downloading a program

When you have found the software you want, you may be asked to type in your name and e-mail address. You should say which operating system you are using, Windows® or Macintosh®.

Most software available for downloading requires Windows® 95 or a later version, or MacOS 7.5 or a later version. If you are not sure that you have the right operating system, look for a link to System requirements, click on it and check. Once you have given all the necessary information, click on the Download link. A window will appear like the one below.

If you use Windows, this window will appear when you start to download a file. Choose the option Save this program to disk.

Saving a program

Select the option *Save this program to disk*, and click on *OK*. Another window will appear, allowing you to choose where you want to save the software you are downloading.

The Save As window

Double-click on this folder to open it.

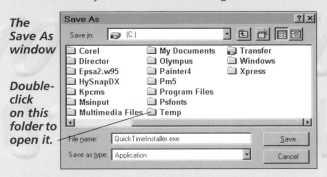

Double-click on the Temp folder, then click on *Save*. You will see a window showing you how your download is progressing. When this window tells you the download is complete, close it.

Installing a program

Close down any other programs you have running. Double-click on the My Computer icon on your desktop, and go to the Temp folder.

You should see a new icon with a file name ending .exe. Double-click on this icon and then follow the instructions you are given to finish installing the software.

If the program was compressed (see page opposite), the filename will have a different ending. Double-click on it to decompress it, and then move the file to the Program Files folder.

Be careful

Always remember that when you download software via the Internet, you can risk downloading a virus or some other element in the program which can damage your computer. If you use a computer at school or at work, always ask your system administrator before you download any software.

How much does the software cost?

Some of the software available on the Web is free. For other software, you may have to pay before you can download it. It should cost no more than if you bought the same product in a store, and there are many excellent programs which cost very little.

 Freeware This is software which is free for anyone to copy onto their computer and use. Sometimes it is a basic version of a program, and you would pay extra for the complete version.

 Shareware You can download this software and try it for free. By doing this, you accept certain conditions. A common condition is that you will pay a small charge for a program if you decide to keep using it after an initial trial period of 30 days. You will then be registered to use the program, and you may be offered a fuller version of the program or free upgrades.

 Trialware You can try out this software for free, but it contains a device which prevents you from using it fully. Some programs have features which don't work. Others contain a built-in timer which stops the whole program from working after an initial trial period. If you decide to keep the program, you pay the company who developed it. They will send you a registration number. This is a code which makes the program work properly.

 Alphaware/Betaware This is new software that needs to be tested. Alphaware is a very early version of a program, and it is generally too risky to try unless you are an experienced computer user. Betaware may still have one or two minor faults, and if you find a fault in a beta program, you should tell the company that created it.

Compressed files

Large program files can take a long time to download, so files are often compressed to take up less space (and less downloading time). You need special software to create a compressed file. You also need the same software to create a full-sized file from a compressed file, before your computer can open the file and run the program. When you have created the full-sized file, you can delete the compressed version.

Two popular compression programs are WinZip® (for PCs) and StuffIt™ (for Macintosh computers). Both of these are available on the Web, at the addresses given in the box on the right.

Sites with software to download

Browser or software manufacturer's home pages:

Microsoft® Internet Explorer:
www.microsoft.com/windows/ie
Netscape®: **www.netscape.com**
Apple: **www.apple.com**

Sites with links to downloads:
tucows.cableinet.net
www.shareware.com
or **shareware.cnet.com**

Compression software:
WinZip® (for PCs) : **www.winzip.com**
StuffIt™ (for Macintosh computers):
www.aladdinsys.com/stuffitlite

Searching the Web

There is a huge amount of information available on the Web, but it can be hard to know where to look for something in particular. However, there are services available on the Web to help you find information. These services are called search engines, directories or indexes.

Directories

Web directories are run by large organizations which collect information about Web sites and arrange them in categories and sub-categories. Categories are connected by hyperlinks, so that you can make your search more and more precise until you have a short list of relevant sites.

Yahoo!® is one well-known directory. You might use it, for example, to look for information on the city of Barcelona. Firstly, type Yahoo!'s URL into your browser's address box. You will see Yahoo!'s home page, as shown below.

Click on the Countries link, in the Regional section to download a page with an index of countries. Click on Spain, and you will download another page with a short list of country subjects. Click on Cities to download an index of towns and cities, and finally click on Barcelona in this index. You will download a page of links covering different areas of interest.

Each time you click on a link, you will download a new page with further links.

This is Yahoo!'s home page for the US.

Click on this link.

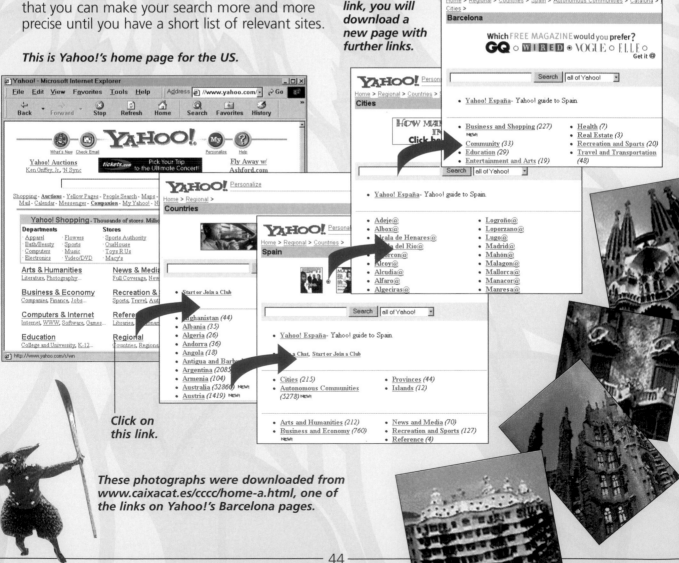

These photographs were downloaded from www.caixacat.es/cccc/home-a.html, one of the links on Yahoo!'s Barcelona pages.

Word searches

If you are looking for information but you are not sure which categories it would relate to, you could try typing a word or a few words in the Search box at the top of the page. For example, if you want to find out about volcanoes, type **volcanoes** in the Search box.

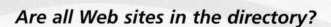

These are some pictures of volcanoes found through a Yahoo! search.

This is Yahoo! UK's home page.

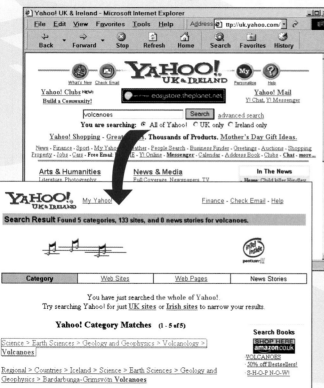

Yahoo! will look for any news articles, categories in its own directory and links to Web sites that relate to volcanoes.

If you want to make a search more precise, type one or two words related to your search subject in the Search box. For example, if you want to find out about volcanoes in Europe, type **volcanoes europe** in the Search box, and Yahoo! will look for sites which contain both terms.

Are all Web sites in the directory?

There are currently over one billion pages on the Web, and so many new sites are being created every day that it is impossible for any directory to list them all. If you can't find the information you are looking for in one directory, try another. If you still have no luck, try an index (see pages 46-47) or a meta-searcher (see pages 48-49).

Missing links

Sometimes Web pages change URLs, and sometimes they are taken off the Web altogether. Directories list so many Web sites that it is impossible for their organizations to keep checking the URLs.

If a site's URL has changed, you may be redirected to the new site automatically, or you may get a message giving the new URL. If the site does not exist any more, you will get an error message. You could try the site again later, in case it is just experiencing a temporary problem with its server. Otherwise, try another directory or an index to see if you can find a more up-to-date URL.

Useful directories

These are some of the most popular Web directories:
Yahoo!® US: **www.yahoo.com**
Yahoo!® UK: **www.yahoo.co.uk**
or **uk.yahoo.com**
Yahoo!® Canada: **ca.yahoo.com**
Yahoo!® Australia: **au.yahoo.com**

Lycos®: **www.lycos.co.uk**

Magellan: **magellan.excite.com**

Go.com℠: **www.go.com**

Indexes

Indexes are the most effective way of looking for a particular word or phrase in a Web site's name or on the site itself.

How do they work?

An index is a program which explores the Web, finding new sites and adding them to its own enormous list of pages. When you use an index, it will scan the list for words matching your search and show you a number of results or "hits" in order of how closely they seem to match.

For example, if you are looking for information about the dinosaur *Diplodocus*, type **diplodocus** in the Search box, and click on Search. Below you will see the first few hits in a popular index called AltaVista®.

Search results

Each item in an index's list of results has a hyperlink to a Web page, and also a little information about the page. The first few entries in the results list will match your search quite closely, but the further down the list you read, the less relevant the links are likely to be.

If you type more than one word in the Search box, most indexes will find sites which contain any one of the words you have typed – giving you a number of hits which aren't relevant to your search.

This is AltaVista's home page.

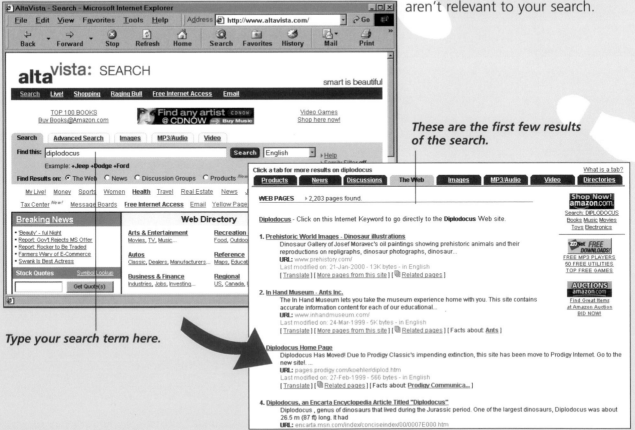

Type your search term here.

These are the first few results of the search.

46

Smart searching

To help you to filter out links to irrelevant Web pages, indexes have tools to make a search more precise.

If you are looking for a particular phrase, you can put it in inverted commas: **"emperor penguins"** will find pages which mention emperor penguins rather than any other kind of penguin – or even any other kind of emperor.

Using operators

You can use shorthand instructions called operators to make your search more specific. Different indexes use different operators, so for best results you should look for the <u>Help</u>, <u>Search Help</u> or <u>Search Tips</u> link on the home page, and read the advice given there. However, most indexes recognize the operators **+** (and) and **–** (not).

+ If you want to search for sites which include several particular terms, not necessarily in the same phrase, type a plus sign before each word in the Search box. For example, if you want to find out about the Vikings in North America, type **+vikings +america** in the Search box. The index will only find pages which include both terms. The more terms you specify, the more precise your search will be.

– You can also exclude terms by typing a minus sign before a word. For example, if you are looking for guitar music but you are not interested in classical music, you would type **+guitar +music -classical**.

Spelling

Indexes will match the exact word you type in the Search box, so be sure to spell words correctly or you may not find the information you are looking for.

If you use capital letters, as in **+Guitar +Music**, most indexes will only find pages which use capital letters in the same places. If you don't include capitals, as in **+guitar +music**, indexes will find pages whether they use capitals or not, giving you many more results.

With some indexes, you can use an asterisk* at the end of a word to look for the same word with different endings. If you type **photograph***, for example, the index will also find pages which mention photographs, photography, photographers and so on.

Indexes

Some of the most popular indexes are:
AltaVista®: **www.altavista.com**

Hotbot®: **hotbot.lycos.com**

Google℠: **www.google.com**
(Google searches work in a slightly different way to AltaVista and Hotbot; read the <u>Search Tips</u> first.)

Expert searching

If you don't find exactly what you are looking for with a directory or an index, there are a number of Web sites and programs which can help you to search a wider selection of sites, or else to make your search more focused.

Meta-searchers

Meta-searchers are search engines which search search engines, giving you the best matches from perhaps a dozen sources. They will only retrieve the first few results from any source, giving you fast results which don't include hundreds of irrelevant sites.

One well-known meta-searcher on the Web is Metacrawler®. Below you can see the results of a search for information on the Republic of Georgia in Eastern Europe. Unlike most indexes, this search did not return numbers of unwanted hits for the state of Georgia in the USA.

The Search Results window in Metacrawler

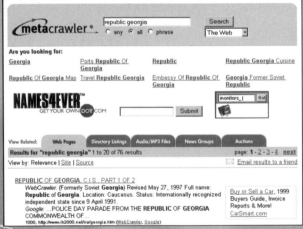

Map of the Republic of Georgia, found on the Web

Ask a question

Sometimes you will get better results if you phrase your search as a question. One search engine which lets you do this is Ask Jeeves™.

The Ask Jeeves home page

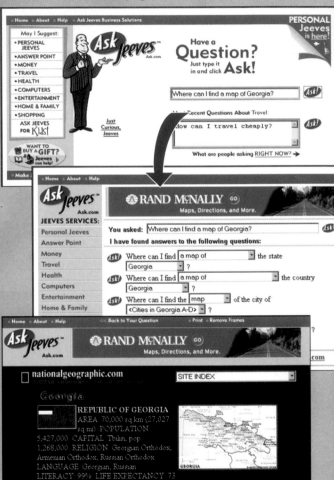

These pages show the results of a search.

You can choose to look at questions asked by other users about particular subjects, or questions being asked by other users while you are looking at the site, to give you an idea how to phrase your question. Once you have asked a question, Ask Jeeves will try a number of search engines to find answers for you.

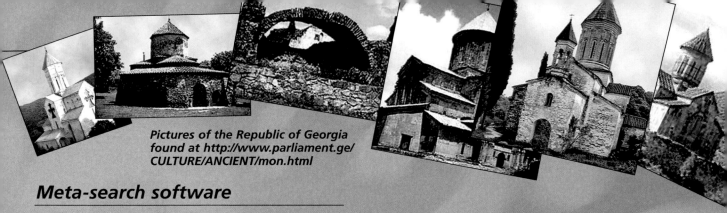

Pictures of the Republic of Georgia found at http://www.parliament.ge/ CULTURE/ANCIENT/mon.html

Meta-search software

Meta-searchers on the Web give impressive results, but there are even more powerful search agents available as software. You can find a program called Copernic® on the Web and install it on your computer free of charge (see pages 42-43 for information on downloading). Macintosh operating system 8.5 and later versions include the search agent Sherlock®, which works in a similar way to Copernic.

Copernic and Sherlock not only search a number of indexes at once, they also assess hits for relevance – how closely they relate to the search terms. This might be based on whether the search terms are included in the Web page's title or description, or how often they appear in the text of the page. Relevance is given as a percentage in a bar reading.

This window appears to show the progress of a search using Copernic.

Search Progress - republic georgia		
Engine	Progress	Matches
AltaVista		0
Direct Hit		10
EuroSeek		0
Excite		10
FAST Search		10
HotBot		0
Infoseek		9
Lycos		0
Magellan		0
MSN Web Search		0
Netscape Netcenter		0
Open Directory Project		0
WebCrawler		0
Yahoo!		0

	Title	Address	Score	Engines
	REPUBLIC OF GEORGIA, C.I.S., PART 1 OF	http://www.ih2000.net/ira/georgia.htm		WebCrawler, HotBo...
	(Formerly Soviet Georgia) Revised May 27, 1997 Full name: Republic of Georgia Location: Caucasus. Status: Internationally recog...			
	Georgia Republic	http://www.dropzonepress.com.../georgia.htm		AltaVista
	Georgia Republic. ~ COUNTRY HAS NO JUMP WINGS ~ CLICK FLAG TO RETURN TO COUNTRY LIST. Dropzone Home Page. Top of...			
	Travel to Georgia	http://www.steele.com/georgia/index.html		Netscape Netcenter...
	Hotel, Banking and Airline information for travelers to the Republic of Georgia. A full service travel agency offers arrangements, h...			
	Georgia Net	http://www.georgia.net.ge/		Magellan, Excite, M...
	Unique searchable collection of georgian resources on the net. Web directory contains the following categories: Art, Business, Co...			
	About Georgia	http://members.tripod.com/ggdav.../index.htm		Direct Hit
	About Georgia (Republic of Georgia). Weather, Currency of Georgian Lari, Map, Flag, Emblem and etc.			
	the Parliament of Georgia	http://www.parliament.ge/		HotBot, Yahoo!, MS...
	the Parliament of Georgia the Parliament of Georgia. You can view a short Guide to the Parliament contains the Constitution and ot...			

These are the first few results of the search, with the search terms highlighted.

This bar shows the hit's relevance as a percentage.

Looking for anything in particular?

There are lots of Web sites to help you look for particular kinds of information. The Websearch page of the directory about.com lists dozens of categories you might use for a search – to find a particular image, for example, or a news item or a person's e-mail address. In each category, you can find links to sites which specialize in searching for the information you want.

Web rings

Web rings are groups of sites with a similar theme. The person or organization which created a Web site agrees to join a ring, and each site in a ring will contain links to all the other sites. Sites such as webring.org have directories of thousands of Web rings arranged by category, so you can browse the directory to find sites which match your interests.

Search agent sites

Meta-searcher sites:
Metacrawler®: **www.metacrawler.com**

Ask Jeeves™: **www.ask.com**

Software to download:
Copernic®: **www.copernic.com**

Sherlock® plug-ins:
www.apple.com/sherlock

Specialist search engines:
About.com Websearch:
websearch.miningco.com

Web rings:
www.webring.org

Portals, hubs and communities

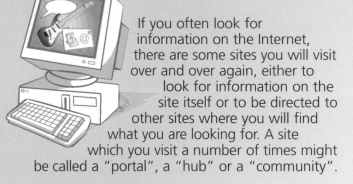

If you often look for information on the Internet, there are some sites you will visit over and over again, either to look for information on the site itself or to be directed to other sites where you will find what you are looking for. A site which you visit a number of times might be called a "portal", a "hub" or a "community".

What is a portal?

A portal is a Web site which acts as a gateway to other Web sites. All directories and indexes are portals, because you use them in order to find and connect to other Web sites. ISP home pages can also be portals if they have links to other organizations' news, information and shopping sites.

There are also a number of specialist portals, which have lots of links to "partner sites" related to a particular subject, such as music. These are sometimes called "vertical portals" or "vortals".

Sportal is a vertical portal dedicated to sports. It has different sites for the UK, France, Spain, Italy, Germany, Denmark, Sweden and Australia.

Click on the Shopping link to go to sites where you can buy sports gear.

What is a hub?

There are some sites which you visit mainly for the up-to-date information you find on the site itself. These sites are known as hubs, and might include online newspapers and television news sites (see pages 52-53), as well as sites which tell you about current developments on the Internet.

At www.zdnet.com you can find news and reviews of the latest Internet technology.

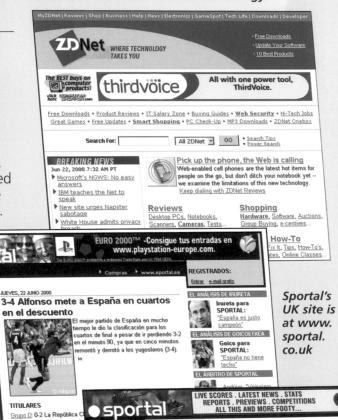

Sportal's UK site is at www. sportal. co.uk

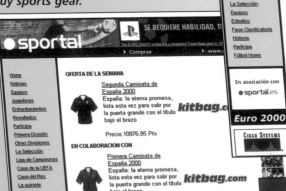

One of Sportal's partner sites is the Benetton Formula 1 motor racing site at www.benettonf1.com

Community sites

Portals and hubs aim to attract lots of regular visitors. One way to do this is to give visitors the chance to say what they think, on bulletin boards or in chat sessions. A bulletin board is a section of a Web site where visitors can post messages about a particular subject for other visitors to read.

Web sites which encourage visitors to have their say are known as communities.

The BBC news page, news.bbc.co.uk, is a popular hub and community site.

Changing your home page

If you visit a particular Web site often, you may like to select it as your home page so that you go directly to that site every time you open your browser. If you are interested in keeping up with the news, for example, you might choose an online newspaper as your home page.

To change your home page in Microsoft® Internet Explorer, click on *Tools* in the Menu bar at the top of your browser window, then click on *Internet Options...* You should see a window like the one below.

The Internet Options window

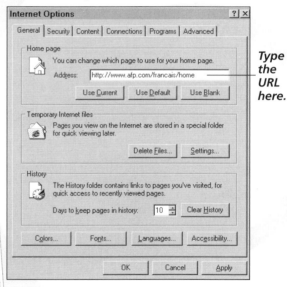

Type the URL here.

Type the URL of the Web site you would like as your new home page in the *Address* box, and then click on *OK* at the bottom of the window. When you click on the *Home* button in your browser's Toolbar, the page you have selected will appear, and when you reopen your browser, it will open onto this page as your home page.

Finding information online

The Web is an excellent place to find up-to-date news or other information. Most national newspapers have online versions, which you can look at free of charge. Television news networks also have their own Web sites, and you can often find out more about the background of news stories which interest you.

Online newspapers

Some of the world's most famous newspapers are available online. You can read the latest news reports, or search the archives for previously published articles.

*This is the online version of the **New York Times**.*

The very latest news

Some online newspapers have a special page for "breaking news" – the latest news stories, which usually come from international news agencies such as AFP. You can also visit the news agencies' own Web sites.

The news agency AFP has news pages in English, French, German, Spanish and Portuguese.

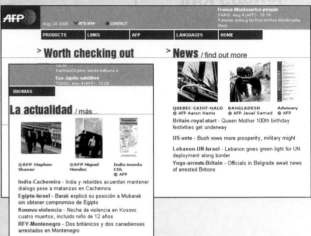

These French, Russian and Italian newspapers are at www.lemonde.fr, www.lenta.ru and www.lastampa.it

The online version of the Guardian has links to pages of sports news, cinema previews and a useful Web guide.

Television networks

You will also find in-depth news coverage at the Web sites of networks such as ITN and CNN. You may be able to listen to sound clips or watch video footage, or have the latest headlines e-mailed to you as the news breaks or at a time you choose.

On television network sites such as CNN's, you can play video clips of recent news stories.

News and reference

Newspapers:
The Guardian: **www.guardian.co.uk**
The New York Times: **www.nytimes.com**
The Washington Post:
www.washingtonpost.com

News agencies:
AFP: **www.afp.com**

Television news networks:
ITN: **www.itn.co.uk**
CNN: **www.cnn.com**

General reference:
Encyclopædia Britannica: **www.eb.com**
Encarta: **encarta.msn.com**

Dictionaries: Oxford English Dictionary:
www.oed.com
Links to dictionaries in other languages:
www.yourdictionary.com

Translation service:
world.altavista.com

Fact finding

If you want to find out more about a topic, you could try looking it up in an online encyclopedia. You can use some encyclopedias free of charge; others will allow you to try a sample search, but you have to pay a small charge each month to use the service in full.

Dictionaries and translations

If you need to look up a particular word, you'll find thousands of dictionaries on the Web, both in English and for other languages. You could also use a translation service, such as Altavista®'s World, to translate text from another language into English.

These are the Search pages of the Encyclopædia Britannica and Quid, an English and a French online encyclopedia.

This translation service can translate from and into half a dozen languages.

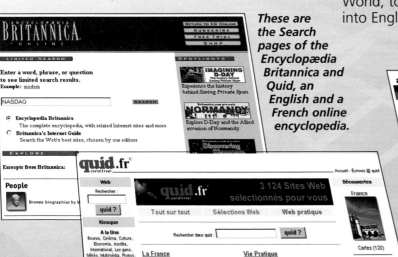

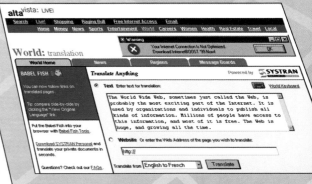

Times and places

As well as news and reference sites, you can find all sorts of other useful information on the Web. You can find out about events in your area and book tickets online. You can also find maps and travel information for cities and countries around the world.

Events guides

The guide *Time Out.com* offers details of music events, theatre, cinema and exhibitions, as well as visitors' guides, for over 30 major cities worldwide.

Time Out.com's home page shows highlights of events in different cities.

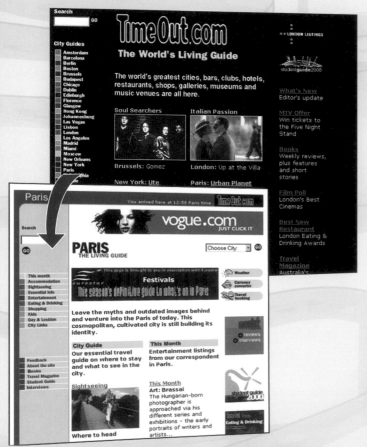

Click on any city in the list on the left of the home page and you will download a page with details of events in that city.

Cinema guides

You can use the Web to read about current film releases, see trailers, read reviews and find out what's on in your area.

At Moviefone, you can read all about the latest film releases. In the US, you can also find details of films showing in your area, check screening times and book tickets online.

Listings

These sites list various kinds of events:
Time Out.com: **www.timeout.com**

Ticketmaster (events around the UK):
www.ticketmaster.com

Evening Standard (in and around London):
www.thisislondon.com

These sites have cinema listings:
Popcorn (UK): **www.popcorn.co.uk**

Moviefone (US): **www.moviefone.com**

Maps

Some listings sites have links to street maps. You can also find specialized map sites which give you details of public transport links, or directions for driving to a place on the map.

This map of the area around the Louvre in Paris comes from the RATP (Paris transport authority) Web site. This site also has maps of subway systems around the world.

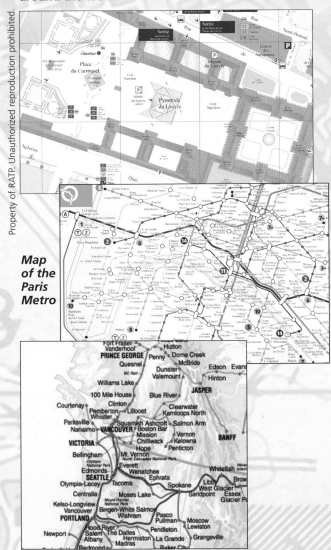

Map of the Paris Metro

This is the US rail network Amtrak's route map for the northwest area.

Maps and transport

Maps:
UK maps: **www.streetmap.co.uk**
US maps: **maps.yahoo.com**
Paris maps and subway plans around the world: **www.ratp.fr**

Timetables:
UK train timetables: **www.railtrack.co.uk**
US train timetables: **www.amtrak.com**

American Airlines: **www.aa.com**
British Airways: **www.britishairways.com**

Timetables

Once you know where you are going, you can find out how to get there with an online timetable. You can find online timetables for most airlines and national rail networks.

This is the home page of Railtrack, the UK rail network. Click on the timetable link to give details of your route, and you will get a choice of train times for your journey.

There are online timetables for the Italian national airline at www.alitalia.it

Museums and galleries

Some of the most attractive sites on the Internet have been created by museums and art galleries around the world. You can explore their collections and look at items in detail, or find out more about a subject or an artist.

Dinosaurs galore

You can find out about dinosaurs and fossils and all kinds of animals and plants at natural history museum Web sites from around the world.

The American Museum of Natural History also has a kids' activity page at www.ology.amnh.org

The page below gives details of an exhibition at the Museum of Natural History in Paris.

A piece of history

You can visit history museums and historic buildings around the world online.

This page tells you about the Grand Trianon at the Palace of Versailles, in France. On the Versailles Web site you can adopt a tree, to help replace the 10,000 trees blown down in the storm of December 1999.

The Imperial War Museum in London is one of a group of six museums represented at www.iwm.org.uk

Museum sites

Natural history:
American Museum of Natural History:
www.amnh.org

Natural History Museum, London:
www.nhm.ac.uk

Palace of Versailles:
www.chateauversailles.fr

In the picture

Many world-famous art galleries have Web sites where you can take a tour of the picture collections, look at pictures in detail, find out about the artists, see details of exhibitions and even visit the gallery shop. Information is usually available in English and other languages.

A selection of gallery Web sites from around the world

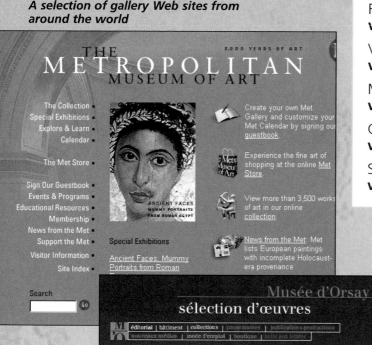

Art galleries

National Gallery, London:
www.nationalgallery.org.uk

Metropolitan Museum, New York:
www.metmuseum.org

National Gallery of Art, Washington:
www.nga.gov

Rijksmuseum, Amsterdam:
www.rijksmuseum.nl

Van Gogh Museum, Amsterdam:
www.vangoghmuseum.nl

Musée d'Orsay, Paris:
www.musee-orsay.fr

Centre Pompidou, Paris:
www.centrepompidou.fr

State Hermitage Museum, St. Petersburg:
www.hermitagemuseum.org

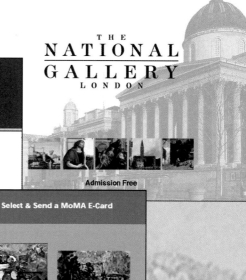

You can send e-cards (e-mail postcards) from the Web site of the Museum of Modern Art in New York at www.moma.org

Music on the Internet

Whether you are looking for information about a band you like, advice on buying a new guitar or music to listen to online or offline, you can find it all on the Internet.

Online music magazines

Many famous music magazines have Web sites packed with news, reviews and sound clips – and if you like what you hear, you will find links to online music stores where you can buy CDs, DVDs and videos.

This is the home page of the UK music magazine NME.

The Ultimate Band List site has news articles and links to official and unofficial Web sites for around a hundred thousand bands and artists.

Your own band

If you play in a band yourself, you will find masses of reviews and discussions of instruments and equipment, as well as links to manufacturers' Web sites, at Harmony Central. There are even pages of advice on starting out as a band, including getting gigs and recording.

Harmony Central's home page

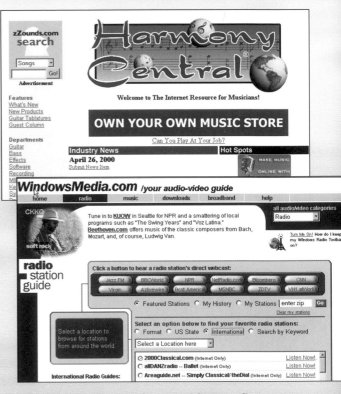

WindowsMedia.com has a guide to radio stations online.

Online radio

Many radio stations broadcast on the Internet, using a process called "streaming". This means that the sound plays directly as your computer receives the data, and the information is not stored on your computer. Streaming technology is often used for sound and video clips, and you need to download a plug-in such as RealPlayer® to watch or listen to them (for information on downloading plug-ins, see pages 42-43).

What is MP3?

Streaming technology (see opposite) is useful when you want to listen to sound clips or radio channels immediately, but the sound quality is not as good as a CD and you can't save copies of what you are listening to. Storing CD-quality sound on a computer takes a lot of memory space, but it is possible to compress files so that they take up very little space without losing much sound quality.

The best-known kind of compressed sound files are MP3 files. You can download MP3 files and play them on your computer using a plug-in (you can download plug-ins from the MP3 Web site itself). You can also use a portable MP3 player.
This is a little like a personal stereo, but instead of cassettes or CDs it uses a memory card. You download MP3 tracks from your computer to the player's memory card. If you like the tracks, you can make a permanent copy on CD.

A portable MP3 player

There are several official MP3 sites where you can find music, mostly by new bands, available to download for free. Established artists also release MP3 tracks from time to time on these sites or their own Web sites.

Copyright

Always remember that music is subject to copyright (see page 39) and that if you make a permanent copy without permission from the copyright holders, you are breaking the law. Several official MP3 sites, such as the MP3 site itself and the Web sites of some record labels, offer "copyright-free" tracks for you to download. Make sure that you only copy tracks from official sites, and that the site states clearly that you have permission to download the tracks you choose.

Neil Barnes, from the band Leftfield, sending out a Webcast from Brixton Academy in London.

Webcasts

Sometimes bands will broadcast a concert on the Internet, filming and recording the concert and using RealAudio® (see page 41) or a similar process to show it on a Web site. Check online music magazines to find details of any Webcasts coming up.

Music sites

Music magazines:
NME: **www.nme.com**
Rolling Stone: **www.rollingstone.com**

Band information:
Ultimate Band List: **www.ubl.com**

Resources for bands and musicians:
Harmony Central:
www.harmony-central.com

Radio stations guide:
windowsmedia.com/radio

Plug-ins:
RealPlayer®: **www.real.com**

MP3 tracks: **www.mp3.com**
and **www.heardon.com**
(Web site of Platinum Entertainment)

Sports online

You can use the Web to keep up to date with sports results, find in-depth coverage of matches, look at your team's Web site, find out about unusual sports, plan sporting holidays and buy equipment.

Sports news

The main television news networks (see page 53) have excellent sports coverage on their Web sites, including the latest results at the time you connect to their site. Some sites' sports pages will update results automatically while you are looking at the page; with others, you can click on the *Refresh* button at the top of your browser window to update the page.

These are the official team sites of Barcelona (www. fcbarcelona.com), Juventus (www. juventus.com) and Chelsea (www.chelseafc.co.uk) football clubs.

League and team sites

You will find official Web sites for all the most popular sports and sporting events. If you don't know a site's URL, you will find lists of links to hundreds of sports sites in a directory such as Yahoo! (see page 44). Yahoo!® lists links for around a hundred different kinds of sport, from archery to windsurfing.

This is CNN/Sports Illustrated's home page.

Sports.com has pages dedicated to different sports in English, French, German, Italian and Spanish.

The Web site of the German premier soccer league (www.bundesliga.de)

Web cameras

Web cameras, or Webcams, are like television cameras connected to the Internet. You can buy a small version to attach to your computer and use at home. You could use a Webcam to record video clips to include in a Web site, for example, or attach to e-mails. You can also visit Web sites to look at the views from Webcams around the world. Usually the images broadcast on the Web are not moving, but are updated about every 30 seconds.

At www.skicentral.com there are links to "snowcams" – Webcams in ski resorts worldwide – so that you can check out the snow before you head for the slopes.

There are some interesting Webcams at:

www.viewsydney.com.au
(views of Sydney Harbour in Australia)

and **www.africam.co.za**
(Webcams in a number of wildlife parks across South Africa).

Winter sports

If you are a skier or a snowboarder, you will find lots of good sites with information about the sport itself, resorts and equipment. You can find holiday offers, and weather reports, as well as news and tips on technique. There are even pages where you can read other people's equipment reviews, or post your own.

Complete Snowboarder.com's home page

Sports sites

Sports news: **cnnsi.com** and **www.sports.com**

Basketball: **www.nba.com**

American football: **www.nfl.com**

Winter sports:
www.complete-snowboarder.com and **www.complete-skier.com**

Shopping on the Internet

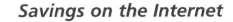

You can buy and sell all kinds of things over the Internet, from books to houses.

Although you may not be able to look at goods or try them out before you buy, shopping sites have lots of ways of giving you information about their products, from customer reviews to 3-D images.

On most shopping sites, you pay for goods using a credit card. If you are under 18, or don't have a credit card, you may have to ask someone else to buy goods for you.

Extracts and sample tracks

Some of the largest online stores are book and music stores. An online store can offer hundreds of thousands of titles, with recommendations, news and reviews and interviews with authors and artists. You can download extracts to read from new books, or play samples of album tracks using a plug-in such as RealPlayer® (see page 41). If you select one title, the store may suggest other similar titles you might enjoy.

These are the home pages of some online book and music stores. Home pages are also called "welcome pages" on some Web sites.

Savings on the Internet

Online stores don't have to pay to keep shops on the high street, so you can often find goods more cheaply online. Although it's hard to choose clothes, for example, without trying them on, you may be able to zoom in and look at them in closer detail, or from different angles. If you are not happy with something you have bought online, many stores will allow you to return it free of charge.

This online fashion store sells clothes much more cheaply than high street stores.

You can click on a Flip Image button to turn an item round and see it from different angles.

BOL and BoxMan have Web sites in English and other languages.

Selecting and paying

Most online stores have a virtual "shopping basket" or trolley or bag, and when you decide you would like to buy an item, you add it to the shopping basket. You can then go back and look around the store site some more, and maybe find more things you would like to buy. You can always change your mind and take an item out of the basket if you decide not to buy it.

When you have chosen all the things you want to buy, click on your shopping basket and click to proceed to a virtual checkout. Here you give your contact and credit card details, and arrange for the goods to be sent to you by post or a delivery service.

Shopping sites

Books:
www.amazon.co.uk
www.bol.com

Music:
www.audiostreet.co.uk
www.boxman.co.uk
www.cdnow.com

Clothes:
www.haburi.com
www.bananarepublic.com
www.tops.co.uk
www.gap.com

Is it safe to shop on the Internet?

Many people are concerned about shopping on the Internet. How can you be sure you are dealing with a reliable company? Is it safe to give your credit card details over the Internet? What happens if something goes wrong, and you don't get the goods you ordered?

Know who you are buying from. As with any kind of shopping, you can take some precautions. Try to deal with established businesses – either companies which also have stores on the high street, or well-known Internet companies. Many Web sites have a page entitled "About us", or something similar, which will tell you more about the company. You can also look for a "Contact us" page, where you can find e-mail addresses and telephone numbers in case you have any questions about your order.

Be careful when giving personal details. Sometimes Web sites will offer you special discounts or gifts to encourage you to visit them again, and will ask for your name and address. You should only give your personal details to well-known, well-established companies.

Use a secure server. Some people don't think it is a good idea to put your credit card details on the Net. It might be possible for criminals to intercept a Web page, take your details and use them to steal money from your account.

In practice, this is rare, especially as most Internet companies use a process called "encryption" to keep your card details safe. When you send your details, they are translated using a special code, so that only the company server can decode them, and the code is different for every transaction.

Some Web sites have a page explaining this process. Otherwise, look for a message telling you that you are about to send information over a "secure server", and a closed padlock symbol at the bottom of your browser window.

Get confirmation of your order. Usually companies will send you e-mail confirmation of your order, and the e-mail may tell you what to do if you don't receive what you asked for. Otherwise, make a note of the details on the "Contact us" page, as mentioned above, so that you can call the company if you need to.

Food, gifts and travel

Shopping on the Internet can make your life easier in many ways. You can use the Internet to order groceries or take-away meals. You can find imaginative presents for special occasions, and have them delivered. Specialist travel sites help you plan a holiday and compare prices, right up to the last minute.

Meals online

You can use the Internet to find recipes and even buy the ingredients. Many grocery stores have Web sites where you can search for recipe ideas and find out about different kinds of food. You can order groceries online, and arrange for them to be delivered to your home.

If you don't feel like cooking, you could use a restaurant directory site to find a restaurant or pizzeria in your area. You place your order online, and then choose whether to collect your meal from the restaurant or have it delivered to you.

This is one UK supermarket which can deliver groceries ordered over the Internet.

Something special

There are lots of sites where you can find great ideas for presents – chocolate and other fine foods from around the world, flowers, jewellery, gifts for the home and more. On some sites you can choose from a list of occasions (birthday, Mother's Day and so on) and types of present, and you will get a list of suggestions for possible presents. You can even type in the date of someone's birthday, and you will get a reminder by e-mail in time for you to choose a present for them.

When you choose a bouquet or a present online, it can be gift-wrapped and delivered with a message from you. Some companies can deliver all around the world.

This French site has a selection of unusual gifts.

You can order take-away meals from this site in the US.

Holidays and travel

Online travel agencies are very popular and offer lots of help in booking travel and holidays. Many rail networks and airlines allow you to book tickets online as well as check timetables at their Web sites (see page 55).

If you are booking airline tickets, there are several online travel agencies which will search for the best fare for you. Type in your journey details and dates and times, and you will get a short list of the best fares available.

These are some online travel agencies.

This site offers deals on flights, holidays, restaurants and gifts at short notice.

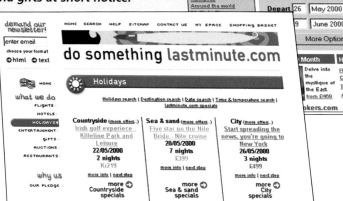

Click on a world map to find out about holidays in that region.

Sites like this one offer a choice of ready-made holidays, or you can plan your own route.

Shopping sites

Grocery stores and delivery services:
www.sainsburys.co.uk
www.tesco.net
www.food.com (delivery in the US)

Gifts:
www.gourmet2000.co.uk
www.giftstore.co.uk

Holidays:
www.ebookers.com
www.expedia.com
www.lastminute.co.uk
www.travelocity.com

Sites such as Travelocity have a "fare finder" to search for the best flight prices available.

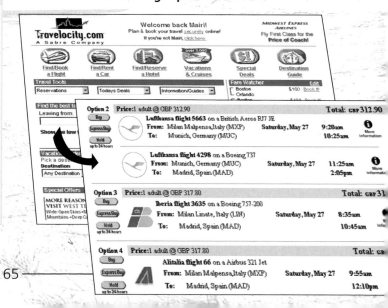

Organizing time and money

You can use the Web to manage your life in all kinds of ways. You will find online banks and investment advice, diary services and virtual money. You can also use the Web to contribute to charities worldwide.

Managing your money

Internet banking can be a very convenient way to manage your finances. You can see your account details 24 hours a day, and arrange to pay bills or take out a loan online in minutes. Online banks use advanced encryption techniques to keep your account details safe (see page 63 for more about encryption).

If you are interested in investing money, you will find lots of information and advice on the Internet, from beginners' guides to highly specialized information. You may have to pay a monthly charge to have full access to some sites, but many sites offer financial information completely free of charge.

Remember that you have to be over 18 to open a current account, to pay by credit card or to sell on the Internet.

These sites offer different kinds of financial services online.

Openbank is a Spanish Internet bank.

Managing your time

You can use a Web diary service to make appointments and send yourself reminders via e-mail. If your friends use the same diary service, you can use the service to contact them and arrange to meet at a time which suits you all – you can all suggest times, and the diary itself will choose one which is convenient for everybody.

This is a diary service called Easy Diary™.

The Motley Fool® site has an excellent beginners' guide to investments.

TheStreet.com offers investment advice in the US.

Virtual money

Most sites which accept payment on the Net rely on credit cards, but there are other ways of paying for goods online. The eCash® payment system, which is highly secure, is supported by banks around the world. You can pay money from your bank account into an eCash account, and then pay for goods online using your eCash currency. Unlike credit cards, you do not have to be over 18 years old to have an eCash account.

Beenz® is a rewards system, a little like "air miles" – you can collect Beenz by visiting different Web sites, or earn them when you buy goods. When you have earned enough, you can use them to buy anything from CDs to holidays.

Helping others

You can find out about charitable organizations around the world on the Internet. One of the most imaginative charity Web sites is the Hunger Site, where you click on a button on screen to send a day's supply of food to a hungry person somewhere in the world. The food is paid for by companies which sponsor the site, and distributed by the United Nations World Food Programme.

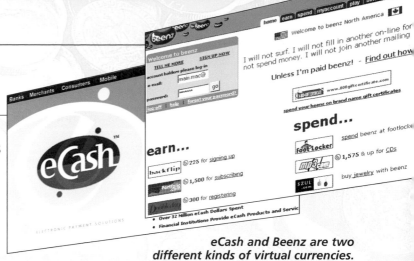

eCash and Beenz are two different kinds of virtual currencies.

Getting and spending

Investment information and advice:
The Motley Fool®: **www.fool.com**
The Street: **www.thestreet.com**
Financial Times: **www.ft.com**
Bloomberg®: **www.bloomberg.com**

Diary services:
EasyDiary™: **www.easydiary.com**

eCash®: **www.ecash.net**

Beenz®: **www.beenz.com**

The Hunger Site: **www.thehungersite.com**

These are the Web sites of some well-known charities.

The Hunger Site arranges donations of food to the starving around the world.

French charity Médecins Sans Frontières has an online scheme to donate meals to Third World countries. Visit www.1francparjour.net or www.paris.msf.org

Games

If you like to play games on your computer, there are lots of them on the Internet to try. There are games you can download onto your computer and play by yourself, or you can join in online games with other players around the world.

Finding games online

The games on the Internet range from traditional games such as backgammon and chess, to 3-D car racing and action games. All of these are "hosted" on computers called servers.

To play, you need to find a server that is hosting the game you want to play. If you know the name of the game you want, you could type its name into a search engine (see page 45). To find a new game, try a directory such as Yahoo!®, where there is a link called "games". Or you could try the shockwave.com site, **www.shockwave.com**, which has links to lots of games.

Many games sites will ask you to register before you play. Read any information that they give you carefully before supplying your details.

Games services

On the Internet, there are also commercial games services. These have their own games servers, which host a wide variety of games. You'll have to pay to use some of them. You can try out demos of new games while you think about buying the full version.

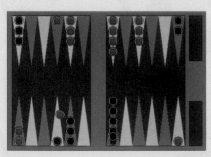

There are many chances to play traditional games, such as backgammon, against other online users. This game is on the pogo.com site.

What software do I need?

To play a game, you often need client software. These are programs that enable your computer to communicate with the server that hosts the game. For example, to play chess, you will need a chess client.

Most games sites on the Internet include hyperlinks. By clicking on these links, you should be able to download all the software you will need to play. A lot of the software available is free, but you will have to pay for some of it. You can find out about downloading software from Internet sites on pages 40-41.

On the Internet there are demos of strategy games, such as Majesty, shown here, that you can download and play.

What hardware do I need?

If you are playing simple card or board games via the Internet, you don't need a powerful computer or extra hardware. However, to play 3-D action games online, you will need a high-speed connection (at least a 56K modem), a fast processor with plenty of RAM (300MHz with 64MB of RAM), a 4GB hard disk and a 3-D video acceleration card. If you are going to play games a lot, you may also want to buy some gaming accessories, such as joysticks, pedals or steering wheels.

Multi-user gaming

One of the most amazing things about the Internet is that you can play games against people in other parts of the world when you're online. You'll find these games, known as multi-user games, on most games sites. You can even play action games against other users if your computer can process the data quickly enough (see below). Some CD-ROMs have a multi-user facility, which allows you to play with other online users who have the same game.

Ping and lag

When you're playing a game online, the actions you make are sent to the server that hosts the game. The time it takes for a signal to travel from your computer to the game server is known as the server's "ping". If the signal travels too slowly, there will be a time-lag before an action you have asked for appears on the screen. This is known as "lag", and it particularly affects gamers playing in countries that are far apart. You can reduce lag by visiting servers that are geographically close to you.

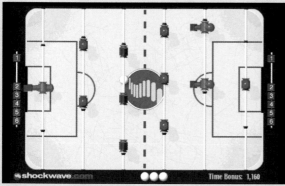

You need quick reactions to play a table-football game called Shockwave® Foosball.

Games consoles and the Internet

Some games consoles now have built-in modems and the capacity to link to the Internet. Users of game machines such as Sega®'s Dreamcast® can connect to the Internet, and play online.

Games on the Internet

Yahoo!® Games: **games.yahoo.com**
Thousands of links at Gamers.com:
www.gamers.com
Multi-user and single user games at MSN® Gaming Zone: **www.zone.com**
More games at Flipside:
www.flipside.com
Traditional games at pogo.com:
www.pogo.com
Links to lots of games at Wireplay:
www.gameplay.com/wireplay
Information about multi-player games at:
www.multiplayer.com
Useful plug-ins at Macromedia®:
www.macromedia.com/software/downloads

3-D games

The graphics used in games are continually getting more complicated, and many games now have amazing 3-D graphics. Because home computers are becoming more powerful, they can process data more quickly, and can display more realistic graphics.

To play 3-D games, you may need to download additional software, but most sites will tell you what you need, and where to find it. There are links to 3-D games on many sites, so have a look, and you're bound to find some.

This 3-D pool game is available at shockwave.com.

Virtual Reality

Virtual Reality (VR) is the use of computers to create objects and places that appear to be real and three-dimensional. In a virtual world (see below), you can move within a "space" as if you were physically inside it. On the Internet, there are many virtual worlds to visit.

Virtual worlds

A virtual world is created using 3-D images. It could be a planet, a room, or even a space containing a single object. It could be a copy of something in the real world, or something completely imaginary. Using your computer, you can explore spaces and move objects within a virtual world.

To visit a virtual world on the Internet, you need to find a site. Try visiting ParallelGraphics at **www.parallelgraphics.com** to find links to lots of virtual worlds.

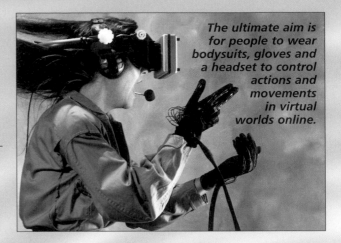

The ultimate aim is for people to wear bodysuits, gloves and a headset to control actions and movements in virtual worlds online.

A VR image of a shuttle orbiter

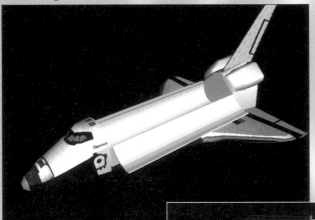

These images are taken from the NASA Web site. Using a mouse, it is possible to move around the objects, to move closer to them and to move further away.

In a virtual world

Entering a virtual world for the first time can be disorientating, but you'll soon find your way around. To move, use your mouse or the arrow keys on the keyboard. You can explore the space all around you and above and below you. To see a different view, right-click the mouse to see a menu. You can alter your view, position, speed, and type of movement.

Wherever you go in a virtual world, it feels as though you are moving. This is because your surroundings on screen change, just as they would in the real world. For example, objects get bigger as you get closer to them.

The computer creates this effect by drawing a sequence of images. In each new image, the objects in front of you are slightly larger than in the previous one.

A space station

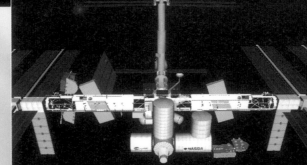

For the feeling of movement to be convincing, the computer has to draw the images quickly.

As a result, the images are often quite simple. However, as data is transmitted more quickly over the Internet, VR worlds will get more complex and realistic.

© The Natural History Museum, London.

These images are from the Web site of the Natural History Museum, London. The VR turtle can be moved around.

Hardware and software

To make the most of virtual worlds on the Internet, you need a powerful computer (at least a Pentium 166 MHz with 64MB of RAM), and a fast modem (at least 56K). You also need a browser, such as Netscape® Navigator 4 or Microsoft® Internet Explorer 4 or a later version, that works with a programming language called Virtual Reality Modeling Language (VRML).

Many technologies, including VRML, are used to create the virtual worlds on the Internet, and they require different plug-ins (see pages 40-41). The only way to find out if your software can handle a virtual world is to visit a site and see what happens. Most sites will tell you if you don't have the correct software and will tell you how to get it. For example, if you don't have a VRML browser, you will need to download a VRML plug-in, which is widely available on the Internet.

MetaStream is an alternative technology that is used for displaying 3-D objects. You can download the MetaStream plug-in by visiting MetaCreations at: **www.metacreations.com**.

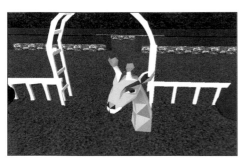

A scene from one of the OnLive! Traveler virtual worlds created using VRML

Meeting people

You can meet other people in virtual worlds on the Internet. A virtual world where you can see and communicate with other Internet users is called a 3-D chat room. To use a 3-D chat room, you'll need to download some software.

Before entering a 3-D chat room, you need to choose an "avatar", which is a character that represents you in the virtual world. It could be a person, an animal, or an imaginary creature. You use your arrow keys or mouse to move your avatar. As you explore, you will see avatars that represent other people who are visiting the virtual world at the same time. In most chat rooms, you type what you want to say, and your words appear on the screen. In some, you can use a microphone to speak to other people.

These avatars are from OnLive! Traveler.

Always be aware that people you meet online may not be who they say they are, and they may say unpleasant things. For information about Internet safety, see pages 116-117.

VR on the Internet

Links to VR sites arranged by subject at:
hiwaay.net/~crispen/vrml/worlds.html
Links to virtual places at Planet 9:
www.planet9.com/indexie.htm
3-D space experiences at NASA:
**spaceflight.nasa.gov/gallery/vrml/
station**

3-D chat rooms at OnLive! Traveler:
www.onlive.com/prod/trav/about.html
Links to virtual worlds at atom:
www.atom.co.jp

Web-based e-mail

When you start an account with an ISP, you are given an e-mail address (see page 18). Many people also choose to set up a Web-based e-mail address. The advantage of a Web-based or online e-mail account is that people can send and receive messages from any computer that has a browser and is online. This is particularly useful to those who travel a lot or for anyone who changes their ISP often. These pages show you how to set up a Web-based e-mail account.

How does it work?

With normal e-mail, messages are held on a computer run by a service provider. You can only access the e-mail from your usual computer because your ISP links your account with your computer. Web-based e-mail is also controlled by a service provider's computer, but it can be accessed by any browser on any computer, using a unique access name and password.

Choosing a service

You will see a list of popular providers in the box on page 73. Many of them provide a free service, which means that you may only have to pay for the time you spend online, not for using the service itself. However, you will probably see advertisements on your e-mails when you use free providers, as this is how they get their money.

Signing up

To sign up for a Web e-mail service, go to the service's Web site by typing its URL into your browser. The exact method of signing up varies, but each site contains a full set of instructions that explain exactly what you need to do.

Filling in a form

When you sign up, most providers will ask you to fill in an online form similar to the one below.

Create Your Yahoo! Email Name   (Already Have One

Yahoo ID: [   ] @yahoo.co.uk

(examples: jerry_yang or filo)

Password: [   ]

Retype password: [   ]

In case you forget your password

If you forget your password, you'll be asked for your birthday, for your code, and to answer one of the questions below. We'll send you a ne password to the email address you provide now, so make sure it is c

This is part of the form that you fill out to sign up for the Yahoo! Mail service.

You'll be asked to choose an access name and a password. The password will allow you to open the mailbox where your messages are stored, and will prevent other people from reading your messages. Choose a password you'll remember. If you do forget your password, some providers, such as Yahoo!®, will ask you a set of questions – for example your birthday or your pet's name. So you may be asked to give this information on the sign-up form. Others, like Excite℠, will ask you to enter a phrase that will remind you of your password.

Um, er, what was my password, again?

excite Sign Up

1. 2. 3. *simple steps gets you* FREE ...

Mail + Clubs + Chat + My Excite Start Page + Portfolio

1. Choose Your Sign in Information - *6-20 characters, only letters, numbers, and dashes.*

Member Name: [   ]

Password: [   ]

Re-enter Password: [   ]

Outside the US? Click here.

2. Password Reminder Phrase - *In case you forget your password.*
Enter a phrase that will remind you of your password. For example, if your password is the l six digits of your social security number, you might enter "the last six digits of my SSN".

Hint Phrase: [   ]

3. Personalization Information- *Information to provide customized features.*
Get local weather reports and events, your horoscope, and other helpful features.
(At Excite we value your privacy and guarantee to adhere to the policies of TRUSTe)

First Name: [   ]

Most service providers ask you to provide a phrase or question, in case you forget your password.

Using Web-based e-mail

To use your Web-based e-mail service, open your browser and type in the URL of the site. Enter your access name and password and your personal page will appear.

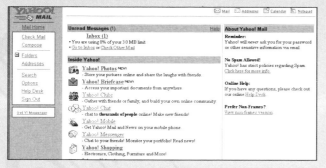

A personal page from the Yahoo! Mail service

You can use it to send and receive messages. Most services offer a spell checker, an address book and some let you send attachments.

The main advantage of Web-based e-mail is its accessibility, and the main disadvantage is that messages can take longer to arrive than those sent using an ordinary e-mail program.

Picking up messages

You can use any online computer to access your messages wherever you are in the world. There are increasing numbers of Internet cafés around the world, which makes it easier to access Web-based e-mail accounts. Libraries, colleges and even shops are other places to try.

You can send and receive e-mail from an Internet café, like this one in Paris.

Providing a service

Here are the Web site addresses of some of the most popular free e-mail providers on the Internet:

MSN® Hotmail®:
www.hotmail.com
Yahoo!®:
mail.yahoo.com
Excite℠:
mail.excite.com
Altavista®:
mail.altavista.com
Bigfoot℠:
www.bigfoot.com
Another.com™:
www.another.com

For advice about free e-mail, and a full list of free e-mail service providers in many countries, visit:
www.emailaddresses.com

Chatting online

Chatting on the Internet means having a typed conversation with one person or a group of people who are online at the same time. Messages appear on screen almost immediately, as it only takes a fraction of a second for them to travel across the Internet. There are several different systems available to help you chat online. Here are just a few.

Internet Relay Chat

With Internet Relay Chat (IRC), people chat to each other in groups called "channels" or "rooms". Each room or channel has a title which covers the main interest of the groups, such as Teen for teenage users.

To take part, you will need an IRC program. Probably the most popular are mIRC for PC users, and Ircle for Macintosh computer users. These programs are available for you to use free of charge for a trial period.

```
<cheeky_babe> saskatchewan                    cheeky_babe
<^goldy^> ?                                    Fixz
<PaperKlip^^> british columbia                 howser
<cheeky_babe> saskatoon                        KristyJane
<cheeky_babe> edmonton                         ldyblueye
<PaperKlip^^> quebec                           PaperKlip^^
<cheeky_babe> vancouver                        pipilongstocl
<^goldy^> canadian                             RITESH
<cheeky_babe> ottowa                           stuhywrt
<PaperKlip^^> nova scotia                      TRUEillusion
<TRUEillusion> im australia how would i know?  ^goldy^
<^goldy^> canada                               ^Pennylou^
<cheeky_babe> ottawa
<MCB> Correct Answers Found:
<MCB> nova scotia Found by: PaperKlip^^
<MCB> quebec Found by: PaperKlip^^
<MCB> british columbia Found by: PaperKlip^^
<MCB> saskatchewan Found by: cheeky_babe
<PaperKlip^^> vancouver
```

An IRC chat session using mIRC in which users in a chat room are quizzing each other about Canadian provinces.

With IRC, you can select a room to enter from a list displayed by your IRC program. During a chat session you will see text written by other users on your screen. To say something yourself simply type it in and press your keyboard's Return key. Your message will appear on your screen and on those of all the other people in the same room.

The mIRC Web site contains full instructions on how to use the program. You'll find more information in the program's Help files.

I seek you

Another popular chat facility is ICQ, which stands for "I seek you". This is a one-to-one chat system. It includes a facility to search the Net for other people who are using ICQ. Some Net users make arrangements to be online at specific times, so that people can find them and chat to them regularly. To use ICQ you will need to download ICQ software (see the box below).

More chat

Both AOL and Microsoft® offer online chat facilities. Microsoft's system is called Microsoft® Messenger, and AOL's is called AOL Instant MessengerSM (AIM). You'll find a *Chat* button on their home pages. One advantage of using the AIM system is that the chat rooms are monitored to ensure that nobody is typing upsetting messages.

You can choose what you would like to chat about from a list of topics. Then you enter the appropriate room. Once inside a chat room, you can just read what is going on (known as "lurking") or join in yourself.

Communication sites

IRC programs: Ircle for Macintosh computers: **www.ircle.com**
mIRC for PCs: **www.mirc.co.uk**

ICQ: **www.mirabilis.com**

AOL Instant MessengerSM: **www.aol.com/aim**

WebPhone: **www.webphone.com**

Video conferencing programs: NetMeeting®: **www.microsoft.com/windows/netmeeting**
Cu-SeeMe: **www.cu-seeme.com**

Web-based chat

There are many different chat sites available on the Web. The advantage of Web-based chat is that you only need to use a browser.

You simply visit a site and join in. Each site will have complete instructions about how to register and use the site.

Some sites, like DoBeDo™, shown below, use cartoons to represent the users in the different chat rooms.

Here are some of the cartoon characters people using the DoBeDo chat site choose to represent them in chat rooms.

The DoBeDo chat site at www.dobedo.co.uk has chat rooms for German and Finnish speakers too.

Safe chatting

Like anything on the Internet, you need to be careful when using online chat. Although it can be sociable and fun, some people write offensive and unpleasant things. Report anything that offends you to the site's managers. There is usually an e-mail link on the site which you can use to contact them. Take a look at the advice on safety on page 116.

Talking on the Internet

There are programs that enable you to speak directly to people via the Internet, like using a telephone. You'll need a sound card, a microphone and speakers attached your computer. You will also need to download a program. There are a selection of programs to choose from. However, the person you want to talk to must use the same program as you.

Talking via the Internet is cheaper than using a phone, because you are only paying the cost of the local phone call to your ISP, even if you are chatting with someone in another country.

WebPhone® made by NetSpeak® allows you to speak over the Internet.

Video conferencing

A video conference is a telephone conversation where you can see the person or people you are talking to. You can use the Internet to do this. As well as a video conferencing program, a microphone and speakers, you will need a Web camera (see page 61).

This is NetMeeting®, conferencing software which is included in the Microsoft® Windows® 2000 operating system.

Newsgroups

Join a discussion group called a newsgroup and get in touch with people who share your interests. From abstract art to zebras, there are newsgroups covering almost every topic. People discuss very little actual news, it's mostly chat and trivia, but it's fun!

What is a newsgroup?

Messages are sent or "posted" to a newsgroup by its members. The messages are stored on a computer called a news server. This computer is maintained by your ISP. Once you have joined a newsgroup, or "subscribed", you can read the messages or send in articles of your own.

What software do I need?

The program you need to use newsgroups, called a newsreader, is included with most browsers. If you have Windows® 95 or a later version, you'll have a newsreader built into Outlook® Express.

Choosing a newsgroup

Follow these steps to choose and subscribe to a newsgroup.

(1) Open Outlook Express and select *Accounts* in the *Tools* menu. In the Internet Accounts window, click on the *News* tab. Select the *Add* button and choose *News*.

(2) A window will open which asks you to type in certain information. This includes your name, your e-mail address and the name of your ISP's news server. Your ISP should have given you this information when you first signed up. If you are unsure, call them up and ask. When you have finished typing the information click on the *Finish* button.

(3) First, a window will appear asking you if you want to download a list of your ISP's newsgroups. Click on the *Yes* button. A window will appear telling you that a list of newsgroups is being downloaded. This will take a few minutes as there are thousands of newsgroups.

(4) A list of newsgroups will appear in the Newsgroup Subscriptions window.

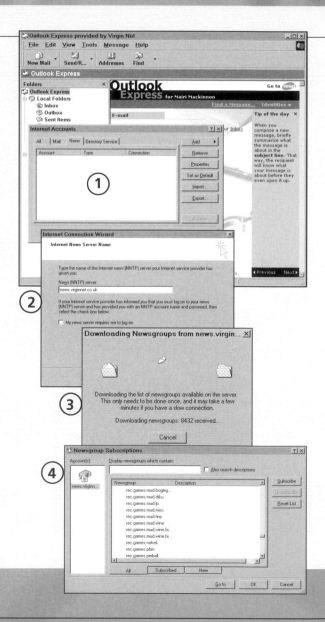

Newsgroup names

Each newsgroup has a unique name. The name acts as a guide to its theme.

The first part of the name describes the category the group belongs to, such as recreational activities or science. Here is a guide to some of the main categories:

comp – computer-related groups

rec – recreational and sports groups

sci – science-related groups

misc – all the groups that don't fit into any other category

soc – groups which debate social issues such as politics, religion or philosophy

The second part of a newsgroup's name narrows down the topic area the group concerns. For example, an imaginary newsgroup name might be **rec.music.presley**. This tells you that the newsgroup is in the recreational activities category, and it is for fans of the music of Elvis Presley.

⑤ To find a group that interests you, type a key word into the "Display messages which contain" box. For example, if you love the *Star Wars* movies, type **starwars**.

Enter your key word here.   **Subscribe** *button*

⑥ Each time you locate a group you want to subscribe to, click on its name in the list. Then click the *Subscribe* button. Finally click *OK*.

⑦ To see a list of the groups you have subscribed to, click on the name of your ISP's news server.

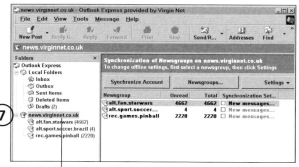

This is the name of the news server.

Posting to newsgroups

As a new member of a newsgroup it's fun to get involved in discussions or ask for information and advice. On these pages you'll find out how.

Articles

The messages sent to newsgroups are called articles or postings. Once you have subscribed to a newsgroup, your news server will send you a copy of all the articles that have been posted to that group in the last few days.

Reading articles

To read the articles in a newsgroup, you will need to open your newsreader program, in this case Outlook® Express. Double-click on the name of your ISP's news server to display a list of the newsgroups to which you have subscribed. Double-click on the name of a newsgroup. A list of articles will appear in the right-hand window. To read one, simply double-click on its subject line in the list. A message window will open.

Outlook Express displaying a list of articles in a newsgroup

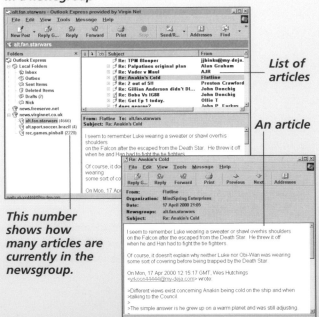

List of articles

An article

This number shows how many articles are currently in the newsgroup.

Keeping track

Once you have read an article, your newsreader will mark it as read. In Outlook Express, read articles are shown in normal type, while unread articles are in bold type. Alternatively, you could just delete any articles you don't want to see again by highlighting their names in the list and pressing the Delete button on your keyboard.

Lurking

When you first join a newsgroup, don't start posting articles right away. Spend a couple of days reading the ones written by other members first, to get an idea of what kind of discussions are currently in progress. This is called lurking.

Frequently Asked Questions

A Frequently Asked Questions (FAQ) article is a message which contains a list of the questions most often asked by new newsgroup members. It saves other members from having to answer the same questions again and again. Most newsgroups have a FAQ article which will appear every couple of weeks. Read it before you start posting.

Ready to post

After you have lurked for a few days, you will be ready to post your own article. You have two main options – you can start a new discussion, known as starting a new thread, or join in an existing conversation by responding to an article.

Starting a new thread

To start a new thread, open Outlook Express and select a newsgroup from the list of the groups to which you are subscribed. Click the *New Post* button on Outlook's toolbar. A New Message window will appear. The name of your news server and the name of the newsgroup will appear at the top of the window.

Type in a title for your article in the *Subject* box, and then type in your message in the message area. When you have finished, click on the *Send* button.

The details of the newsgroup are filled in automatically at the top of the message window.

News Server:	news.virginnet.co.uk
Newsgroups:	alt.fan.starwars
Cc:	
Subject:	Meaning of name Darth Vader

Joining in a discussion

An existing thread consists of an initial message, such as "Ronaldo is the greatest soccer player in history", followed by responses from other members of the newsgroup. The initial message should be displayed in your newsreader with a "+" icon beside it. If you click on this symbol, a list of the articles in the thread will appear. The responses in the thread should have the same subject line with "Re:" in front of it.

To join in, open the message you want to respond to, following the method described on page 78. You have two choices: you can send a message to all the members of the newsgroup (called following up), or just to the person who wrote the article.

To follow up, click the *Reply Group* button on the toolbar of the window in which the article appears. A New Message window will open, with the details of the newsgroup filled in and the same subject line as the message you are following up. Type in your article.

To reply directly to the author of an article, press the *Reply* button and follow the same process as described above. Your reply will not be sent to all the other members of the newsgroup.

Creating your own Web site

Why not tell the world about yourself by creating your own pages and putting them on the Internet for everyone to see? The easiest way of doing this is to use a program called a Web editor.

A Web editor

Web pages are produced by using a computer code called HTML, which converts ordinary text documents into Web pages. The advantage of a Web editor is that it automatically produces the HTML code which turns documents into Web pages, so you don't have to type it in yourself. The most popular type of Web editors are known as WYSIWYG Web editors.

WYSIWYG stands for "What you see is what you get". As you build Web pages, a WYSIWYG Web editor shows you what they will look like when viewed through a browser (see page 34), allowing you to design your document as you go along.

With a WYSIWYG Web editor, you start by typing some text into a blank document. You can insert files created in other programs, such as pictures or sounds, whenever you want to.

Once you have created a basic page, you can easily reorganize the information on it. There are various buttons and menu items that you can use to improve your page's appearance. For example, to change the way a word looks, you can select it with your mouse and click on a button that makes it **bold**.

The examples in this book are created using a Web editor called Microsoft® FrontPage® Express, but if you are using a different Web editor, such as Netscape® Composer, you will find that the procedures involved are very similar.

A WYSIWYG editor called Microsoft® FrontPage® Express

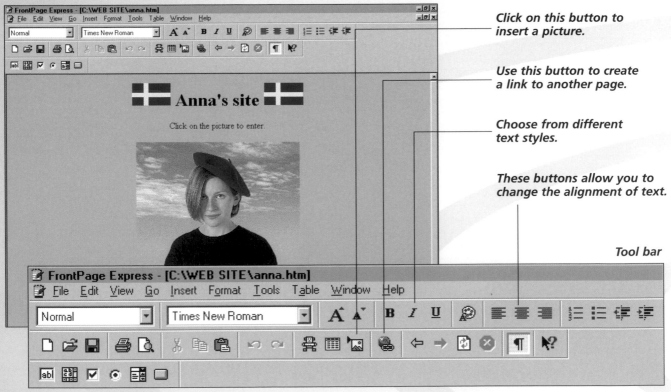

Click on this button to insert a picture.

Use this button to create a link to another page.

Choose from different text styles.

These buttons allow you to change the alignment of text.

Tool bar

Choosing a Web editor

Different Web editors have different advantages and disadvantages. FrontPage Express, for example, has all the tools you need to build great Web pages, but it is designed to work with the Internet Explorer browser. This means that the HTML code it produces can be hard for other browsers to read, and some features of your Web pages may not work when viewed through a different browser.

Professional Web designers often build pages using an editor called Macromedia® Dreamweaver® which produces very "pure" HTML code that any browser can read.

A Web editor called Macromedia Dreamweaver

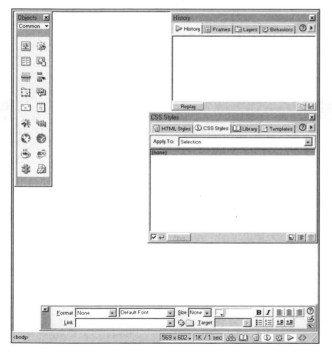

Advanced Web design

Macromedia also sell a Web graphics package called Fireworks®, which allows you to create your own buttons and animations for your Web pages. It is available from the Macromedia Web site (see box).

Obtaining a Web editor

Some Web editors are free of charge. For example, the editor we have used in this book, Microsoft FrontPage Express, comes free with Microsoft's browser, Internet Explorer. There are also many Web editors that you have to pay for, but you can try out most of them free of charge for a limited period of time. Macromedia, for example, offers you a free 30 day trial period of the full Dreamweaver program (to download the trial version of Dreamweaver, visit the Macromedia Web site, at the address below). At the end of the 30 days, you are given the option to buy Dreamweaver.

It is a good idea to test several different programs and decide which one suits you best before you spend any money.

Web editors on the Internet

For Microsoft® Windows® and Macintosh computers: Macromedia® Dreamweaver®:
www.macromedia.com
Adobe® GoLive™:
www.adobe.com

For Windows:
Microsoft® FrontPage® Express:
www.microsoft.com
Netscape® Composer:
home.netscape.com

For Macintosh computers:
BBEdit:
www.barebones.com

Planning your Web site

Before you start building a Web site, you should plan it carefully. Decide what sort of information you are going to include, and how you are going to organize it. Before you use your computer, jot down your ideas on paper so that you can work out the best way of presenting them.

⚠ Be safe

Millions of Internet users will be able to see the information on your Web site. Don't include anything private, such as your home address or telephone number.

Decide on content

With the Internet, you aren't restricted to using words to share information with other people. You can use sounds and pictures too. For example, if you are a musician, you could include a short recording of your music.

If you belong to a club, you could use photographs to introduce its members, or to show the sort of activities it arranges. You could also add a chart detailing future events.

You can also include pictures created on a computer to decorate your Web pages. Pictures created on a computer are known as computer graphics.

Organize content

Decide how many pages your Web site is going to contain and divide up your content between them. Give each page a title which indicates the information it will contain, for example, "About myself" or "Sports and hobbies". This will help you decide where each piece of information fits best.

How long?

Don't try to put too much information on one page. There should be enough content to fill at least one screen. But if you have to scroll down more than two screens to reach the bottom of a page, you should divide up the information into a few shorter pages instead.

You will find instructions for adding extra pages to your Web site on page 87.

Here are some of the things that you can include on your Web site.

Photographs – Find out how to include photographs on page 96.

Sounds – Find out how to insert sounds on page 100.

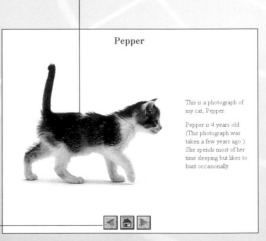

Backgrounds – Discover how to add attractive backgrounds on page 90.

Hyperlinks – Page 99 explains how to include picture links.

Design a layout

It is a good idea to design your Web site on paper first. Making sketches like the ones shown above will help you decide where to put pictures in relation to text.

Include a home page

Once you know what you are going to put on your site, you can plan a home page. This will be an introductory page which tells visitors what information your site contains. It can also include information such as when the site was built or updated.

A home page

This picture links to a page about music.

This one links to a page containing photographs.

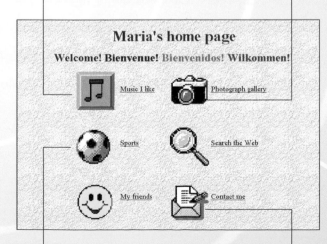

Maria's home page
Welcome! Bienvenue! Bienvenidos! Wilkommen!

 Music I like   Photograph gallery

Sports   Search the Web

My friends   Contact me

Follow this link to see a page about soccer.

Click here to send a message to the creator of the site.

The home page is the first part of your site people will see, so it has to be eye-catching. These home pages show you what the sites are about, and make you want to find out more.

TERRY'S TIGER WORLD

Welcome to my site devoted to these beautiful creatures. If, like me, you are interested in the behaviour and habitats of one of the world's most endangered species, then you will find plenty of information here to help

joe's cool dance site

Clubs   Events

BIKES! BIKES! BIKES!

Click here to enter

Paradise Health & Fitness Club

Using a Web editor

These pages will show you how to create your Web pages using Microsoft® FrontPage® Express.

Getting started

FrontPage Express comes with Microsoft® Internet Explorer, so it should be stored in the same folder on your computer.

When building a Web site, the first thing you need to do is construct a home page.

FrontPage has a tool called a *Wizard* to help you do this. It takes you through a set of questions, then sets up a framework for your home page. The steps below show you the type of questions you will be asked by the Wizard.

Using the FrontPage Wizard

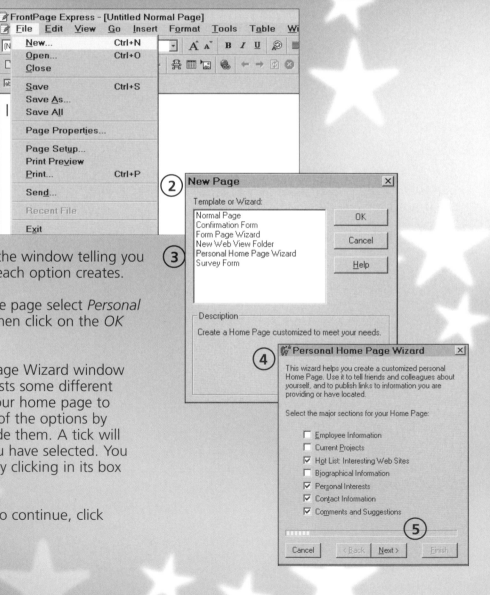

(1) To open the FrontPage Wizard, click on *File* in the tool bar to open the drop-down menu and select *New*.

(2) The New Page window will appear. To find out more about the options available in this window, click once on each of the items in the *Template or Wizard* list. Information will appear at the bottom of the window telling you which sort of Web page each option creates.

(3) To work on your home page select *Personal Home Page Wizard*, then click on the *OK* button.

(4) The Personal Home Page Wizard window opens. This window lists some different sections you may want your home page to contain. Select any or all of the options by clicking in the boxes beside them. A tick will appear in those boxes you have selected. You can deselect any option by clicking in its box again.

(5) When you are ready to continue, click on the *Next* button.

6 A window will appear asking you to give your Web page a name. The *Page URL* refers to the name of the HTML file your Web editor is creating, so you do not need to change it. The *Page Title* is what will appear at the top of any browser viewing your page, so type your name followed by "home page" into the *Page Title* box. Click the *Next* button when you are ready to move on.

7 Depending on the options you selected at stage 4, a series of windows will now appear asking you how you would like each feature of your site to be presented. In each case select an option, then click on *Next*.

8 Finally, a window will appear asking you to specify the order in which you would like your Web page features to appear. To move an item up or down the list, click on it. Then, when it is highlighted, click on *Up* or *Down* to move the item through the list. When you are satisfied with the order of your list, click on *Next*.

9 A final window will appear. Click on *Finish*, and FrontPage Express will generate a home page framework for you.

10 A basic home page will appear in your FrontPage Express window. To see how to save it, turn to page 86.

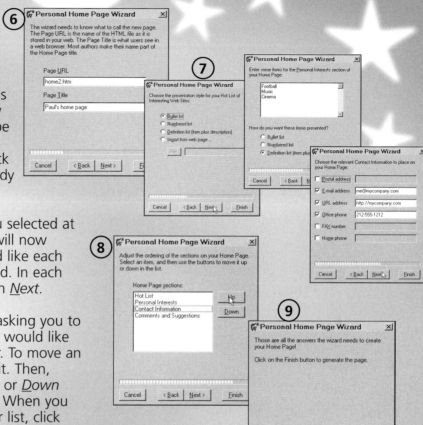

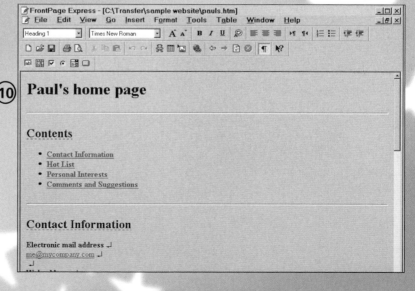

Saving and opening Web pages

While you are working on your Web site, you should save any pages you create regularly. Each page needs to be saved as a separate file. Once you start adding pictures to your site (see pages 96 to 97), they will need to be saved as separate files as well. You should create a new folder on your computer for storing all your Web page files.

Saving pages

(1) To save a Web page created in FrontPage® Express, click on *File* at the top of the FrontPage Express window. Then click on *Save As*.

(2) A Save As window will appear. Give your page a name in the *Page Title* box, then click on the *As File* button.

(3) A Save As File window will appear. Click on the arrow next to the *Save in* box and choose where you want your Web site folder to be saved.
   If you are saving your home page, you should name the file either index.html or default.html, as these are the file names browsers will look for first when they locate your Web site.

(4) Click on the *Create New Folder* button.

(5) A new folder will appear in the window. Call the folder "Web site", followed by your name. Then click on *Save*.

In future, you should save all newly created files for your Web site into this folder.

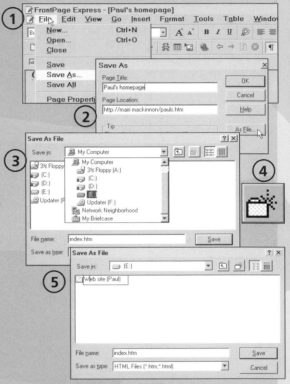

Opening saved Web pages

(1) To open a Web page you have already saved, open FrontPage Express and click on *Open* in the *File* menu.

(2) An Open File window will appear. Click on the *Browse* button.

(3) Click on the arrow next to the *Look in* bar. Double-click on your Web site folder and then select the file you wish to open.

(4) Click on *Open*. The page you want to open will appear in the FrontPage Express window.

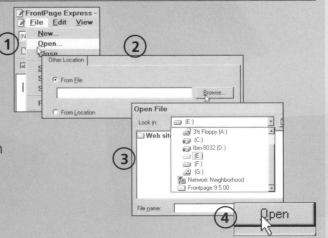

Rearranging Web pages

Don't let a Web page get too long. Long Web pages make it hard for visitors to find the parts that interest them, and scrolling through them is both boring and frustrating. To avoid this you should present different subjects on your site on different pages. This will help to make your site clear and easy for visitors to find their way around.

Adding pages

To create a new Web page, follow the instructions below.

(1) In FrontPage Express click on *File*, then click on *New*.

(2) In the New Page window, select *Normal Page* and click on the *OK* button. A blank page will appear. See page 86 for instructions on saving your new page.

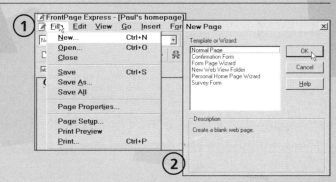

Moving information

(1) To move information to a new page, first highlight the section of your page that you want to move (see page 88).

(2) Open the *Edit* menu and click on *Cut*. The selected area of the page will disappear.

(3) Open the page you want to move the section to (see page 86), and position your cursor at the top of the area where you want it to appear. Open the *Edit* menu, then click on *Paste*. The section you cut will reappear on the new page.

For information about linking your pages together, see pages 98-99.

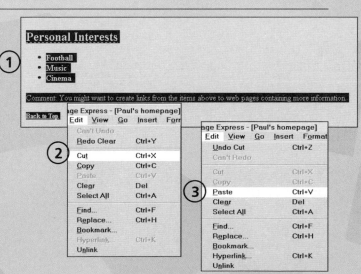

Changing text

You can change the appearance of the text on your Web page using the FrontPage® Express format toolbar.

Selecting text

To alter the appearance of a piece of text you need to select it. To do this, click on the beginning of the text and, while keeping your finger on the left-hand mouse button, run your cursor down to the bottom right-hand corner of the text. It will now be highlighted.

This piece of text has been selected.

To alter it you will need to use the tools on the FrontPage Express format toolbar, shown here.

Change Style box

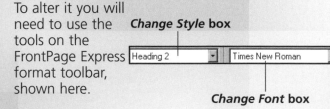

Italic tool

Bold tool   **Underline tool**   **List tools**

Text Size tools   **Align tools**

Change Font box   **Text Colour tool**   **Indent tools**

Changing fonts

Select the text you wish to adjust, then click on the fonts box in the top left-hand corner of your screen. A list of fonts will appear. Select one by clicking on it and your text will change accordingly.

These are just some of the fonts you can use.

Courier

Handel Gothic

Times

Zapf Chancery

Select your fonts from the fonts box.

Changing text size

Select the text you wish to adjust, then use the *Increase Text Size* and *Decrease Text Size* tools.

Increases your text size

Decreases your text size

Creating different text effects

Select some text and experiment with the other tools along this toolbar by clicking on them.

 Makes your text italic

 Makes your text bold

 Underlines your text

Correcting mistakes

If you don't like something you've done, FrontPage Express allows you to correct mistakes using the *Undo* and *Redo* tools. Clicking on *Undo* will remove the last adjustment you made. Clicking on *Redo* will add it again.

Undo   **Redo**

Typing text onto your page

To type new text onto a Web page, just position your mouse pointer where you want the text to appear and click on the left-hand mouse button. A cursor will appear and you can start typing.

Creating lists

FrontPage Express has a feature which helps you to create lists. You can also turn the items on the lists into hyperlinks to other Web pages (see page 99 for instructions on creating hyperlinks).

(1) Type in the items you want to be included in your list.

(2) Select your entire list (see Selecting text on the previous page for a description of how to do this).

(3) Click on the arrow beside the *Change Style* box in the top left-hand corner of the screen. A menu will open.

(4) Select *Numbered List*. Your selected text should change accordingly.

(5) To use bullet points instead of numbers, select *Bulleted List.* You can click on any of the different options in the drop-down menu while your text is highlighted to see what they do.

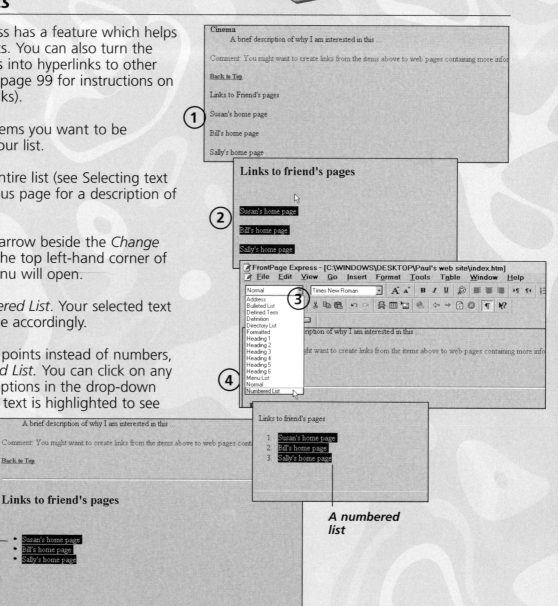

A bulleted list

A numbered list

Adding colour

Unless instructed otherwise, a browser will display text in black on a grey or white background. To make your Web site look more attractive, you can specify different colours for the background and the text. Colours help to separate the information on a page, making it easier for visitors to read.

Describing colours

A computer describes colours using combinations of letters and numbers known as hexadecimal colour codes. These codes are always made up of six characters. For example, the code 000000 describes black. People designing Web pages in HTML have to include hexadecimal codes to tell the browser which colours to use. With a Web editor you simply choose the colours from a menu, and the editor writes the colour codes for you.

Choosing colours

Choosing the colours for your Web page is easy using FrontPage® Express:

①Click on *Format* in the menu bar to open the drop-down menu. Then click on *Background*.

②The Background window will appear. The five boxes containing colours in the middle of the window specify the default colours for different aspects of your Web page.

③To change the colours, click on the arrow by the box titled *Background* to open the drop-down colour menu. Select the colour you want by clicking on it. Click on *OK*.

④The background colour of your Web page will change to the colour you selected.

You can also use the Background window to change the colour of your text and hyperlinks. Simply follow the above procedure, replacing *Background* at stage 3 with the aspect you want to change.

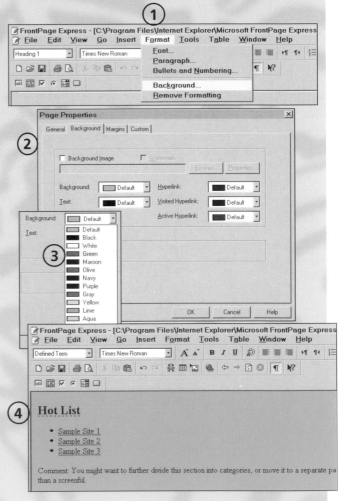

Colour advice

It is fun to experiment with different text and background colours. However, before you settle for a particular combination, make sure that all the text on your page is easy to read. Dark colours, such as navy blue or black, look good on a white or pastel background. Light colours, such as white or yellow, show up clearly on a dark background.

Avoid large amounts of very bright colours such as red or shocking pink. People may not bother to explore your site thoroughly if you make it difficult for them to read the information it contains.

It is difficult to read green text on a red background.

Blue text on a yellow background is easy to read.

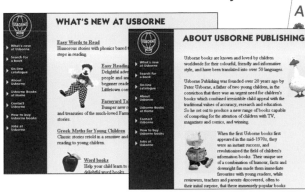

The Usborne Publishing site at www. usborne.com uses blue and black text on a yellow background.

Design tips

Many people think that the best sites on the Internet use white text on a black background or black text on a white background. If you choose one of these combinations, you should use striking, colourful pictures to brighten up your site (see pages 92-97 for advice on adding pictures).

The pictures on these Web pages help to break up the text and make the layout more appealing.

Equipment differences

If you are using a Macintosh computer to design your site, remember that they show colours differently. A Web page designed on a Mac will appear slightly duller on a PC.

Pictures on Web pages

One of the reasons the Web is such a popular source of information is because it contains pictures. Here are some of the ways in which pictures can be used on a Web site.

A picture gallery

Some Web sites contain a gallery section where pictures are displayed. This may include a page of "thumbnails", which are small versions of the images that are displayed elsewhere on the site. If you decide you want to see a larger version of a picture, you can click on its thumbnail to download it.

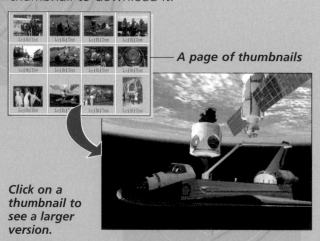

— *A page of thumbnails*

Click on a thumbnail to see a larger version.

Decorative dividers

Long, thin pictures, known as bars, can be used to divide up different sections of information on a Web page.

A bar has the same function as a rule, but looks more interesting.

Artists' materials

Pencils

Pencils should form the basis of your drawing kit. They are cheap and are available with a variety of leads, from very hard (9H) to very soft (9B).

Soft leads, from 9B to B, give dark lines and are useful for dark shading. B stands for black. The higher the number, the softer and more smudgy the lead.

Hard leads, from 9H to H, are useful for creating precise lines and light shading. H stands for hard. The higher the number, the harder the lead.

Charcoal and chalk

Charcoal and chalk both mark paper easily, so they are ideal for creating bold, loose sketches and effects.

Both charcoal and chalk tend to smudge. Use a spray-on fixative as soon as you have finished a picture. Spray-on fixatives are available from most art shops.

Backgrounds

You can use computer graphics to create attractive backgrounds. A background is usually made from a small graphic, called a tile, that a browser displays over and over again.

Patterns that don't distract your visitor's attention from the text, and that fit in well with the theme of the page, look best.

The page below has a background that looks like water.

This tile is repeated to create the background.

Indicate links

A picture can be a hyperlink to another Web page. For example, pictures of houses, such as the ones shown here, are often used as hyperlinks to a site's home page. Whenever you pass your mouse pointer over a hyperlink, the pointer turns into a hand.

A selection of home page icons

Obtaining pictures

There are many pictures on the Internet that you can copy and include on your site. You can find collections of backgrounds, bars, buttons and icons. To do this, use a search engine to carry out a keyword search.

You will find instructions for copying pictures from the Internet on page 39.

You will find these icons at www.aplusart.com

Free pictures

If you find any other picture collections, make sure the pictures are available for public use before including any of them in your site. Some pictures, known as public domain pictures, are not copyrighted.

For more information about copyright, see page 39.

A selection of copyright free images from NASA

Digital pictures

You may want to include your own drawings or photographs on your site. If you have a digital camera, you will be able to transfer pictures directly to your computer as digital images. Other pictures need to be recorded in digital code first.

Pictures can be converted into digital code by a machine called a scanner. This process is

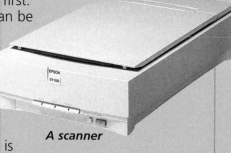

A scanner

called scanning in. You can find out more about it on page 94.

Top-quality scanners cost a lot of money, but you can buy one which is perfectly good for home use fairly cheaply. If you don't want to buy a scanner, you can have your pictures scanned at most photocopying shops or photograph processing businesses.

Useful sites

Backgrounds:
www.netscape.com/assist/net_sites/bg/backgrounds.html

Pictures and icons:
www.w3.org/Icons
www.nasa.gov

Image-editing software:
For Microsoft® Windows®:
LView: **www.lview.com**
JASC®'s Paint-Shop Pro™: **www.jasc.com**
For Macintosh computers:
GraphicConverter:
www.graphicconverter.net

Preparing pictures

When you scan in a picture, you create an image file that you can insert into a Web page. This section explains how to create image files and adapt them for use on the Internet.

How does a scanner work?

A scanner is attached to a computer. Software on the computer tells the scanner how to collect and save information about a picture. This software is known as image-editing or imaging software.

The scanner divides a picture into tiny dots known as picture elements or pixels. It gathers information about the colour and position of each one. It then records this information in digital code so that the computer can reproduce the picture. You use imaging software to tell a scanner how many pixels to divide a picture into. The number of pixels in an image is known as its resolution. It is usually measured in dots per inch (dpi).

Pixels

When you look at a digital image close up, the pixels are clearly visible.

Imaging software also lets you alter or edit digital images, and create images from scratch. You can find out how to obtain an image-editing program on page 93.

File size

When creating picture files for use on the Internet, it is important to make them as small as possible so that they download quickly. The size of a file is measured in bytes.

Resolution

You can control the size of an image file by changing its resolution. A "high-resolution" image contains a lot of pixels so it produces a large file. A "low-resolution" image contains fewer pixels so it is contained in a smaller file.

You can see the difference between a high-resolution and low-resolution image when you print them out.

Compare the quality of a high-resolution picture to the quality of a low-resolution picture.

This is a high-resolution image. It was scanned in at 350 dpi.

This is a low-resolution image. It was scanned in at 72 dpi.

High-resolution and low-resolution images look very similar on a computer monitor. When you prepare a picture for use on the Internet, scan it in at 72 or 75 dpi. Low-resolution images are good enough for use on the Internet.

Saving pictures

Imaging software can save pictures in many different ways. The most popular types of picture files used on the Internet are Graphical Interchange Format (GIF), Portable Network Graphics (PNG) format, and Joint Photographic Experts Group (JPEG) format.

GIF

GIF files are often used for pictures that have large areas of one colour with no shading. For example, most icons, buttons and bars are GIF files.

These icons from the Chicago Museum of Science and Industry's site are GIF files.

GIF files contain a maximum of 256 colours. This helps to make the files small. If a picture contains more than 256 colours, an imaging program reduces the number of colours to save it as a GIF. When you save a picture as a GIF, add the extension .gif to the file name.

PNG

PNG (pronounced ping) files are used as an alternative to GIF files for graphic images. PNG files have several advantages over GIF files. Images stored in PNG format are up to 30 percent smaller than GIF files, and they are not limited to 256 colours. However, they do not support animation (see page 102). PNG files are less common than GIF and JPEG files (see right) and some browsers will have trouble displaying them, but their popularity is growing. If you save a PNG file, add the extension .png to the file name.

This picture of the Chicago Museum of Science and Industry (www.msichicago.org/) is a JPEG file.

JPEG

JPEG files are ideal for pictures that contain many colours, such as photographs. They record the information in a way that makes the file smaller. This is called compression.

JPEG files can be compressed by different amounts. The greater the amount of compression, the smaller the size of the file. However, the amount of compression also affects how good a picture looks. The smaller the amount of compression, the better the quality of the picture.

Try compressing a file by different amounts until you find the smallest file that still looks good. To do this, first save a few different versions of an image by altering the amount of compression each time. When you save a JPEG file, add the extension .jpg to the file name.

A dialog box from an imaging program called Adobe® Photoshop®.

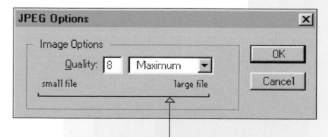

Move this slider to the left to compress the file.

Next, open up all the versions at the same time in your imaging program so that you can compare what they look like. Try to keep all your picture files under 30 kilobytes (KB).

Putting pictures on Web pages

Adding an object, such as a picture or a sound, to a Web page is known as embedding. This section tells you how to embed pictures.

Embedding a picture

Imagine, for example, you want to use Microsoft® FrontPage® Express to embed a picture called "surfer.jpg" in a Web page.

Before you do anything else, you should store a copy of the image in your Web page folder (see page 39 for instructions on saving images). Here's what you do next:

①Position your cursor where you want the top left-hand corner of the image to be on your Web page. Click on *Insert*. A drop-down menu will appear.

②Select *Image* in the drop-down menu. An Image window will appear.

③Click on the *Browse* button. A second Image window will appear.

④Click on the arrow next to the *Look in* box and select the file name of your image from the hard drive by clicking on it.

⑤Click on the *Open* button. The image will appear on your Web page.

When you click on Open, FrontPage Express will import your image onto the page below the cursor.

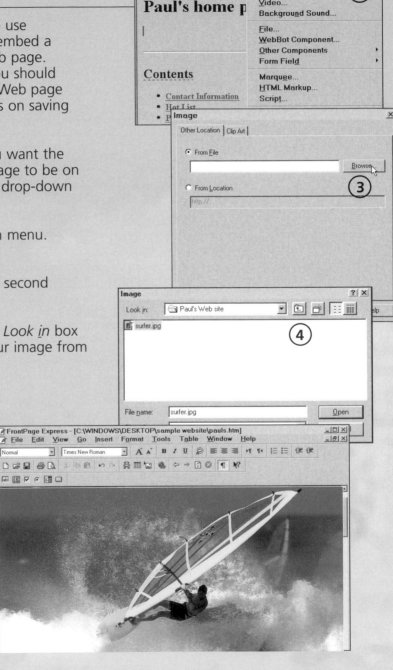

Arranging pictures

To arrange pictures on your Web page using FrontPage Express, click on the picture to select it and then use the Align tools in the format toolbar to change its position.

These are Frontpage Express' Align tools.

Align Left   Center   Align Right

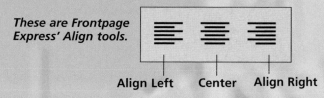

The picture on this page is aligned right. Notice how it pushes the text to the left.

If you have text next to a picture, FrontPage will not allow you to *Center* your picture. You have to move the text first, so that it appears either under or above the picture.

When a picture appears in the middle of a Web page, it pushes the text down.

Reusing pictures

It is a good idea to reuse pictures wherever possible. This brightens up a site without increasing the time it takes to download. This is because when a browser downloads a Web page, it copies each piece of information onto your computer. When a picture appears for a second time, the browser displays the copy that is stored on your computer. It doesn't have to get the information from the Internet again. Don't re-use pictures too often though, or your Web site will look dull.

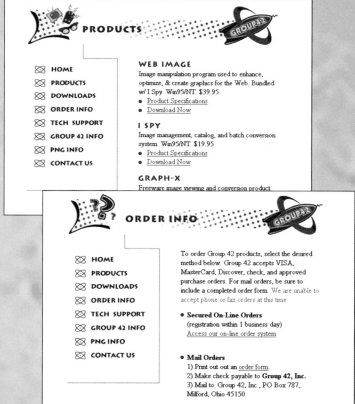

Several of the pictures on the site above are repeated.

Remember that pictures can take a long time to download. Visitors will lose patience and give up if your Web pages take too long to appear.

Linking Web pages

Once you have created a few Web pages, you should join them together with hyperlinks. You can also link your pages to other people's sites.

You can make both words and pictures into hyperlinks. For example, you could make a hyperlink to the White House Web site from the sentence "Last year, my family and I visited the White House" or from a photograph of the White House.

Links within a site

Links within a Web site are called local links. They help visitors to find their way around the pages on the site. Ideally, each of your pages should contain a link to your home page, as well as a selection of links to other pages on your site.

This picture shows how you can use hyperlinks to jump from one Web site to another.

Links to other sites

Links to other sites are known as global or remote links. You can use remote links to connect your page to other pages on the same subject or to direct your visitors to sites you have enjoyed.

These links are part of the text.

A local link

A list of interesting and useful sites is called an index.

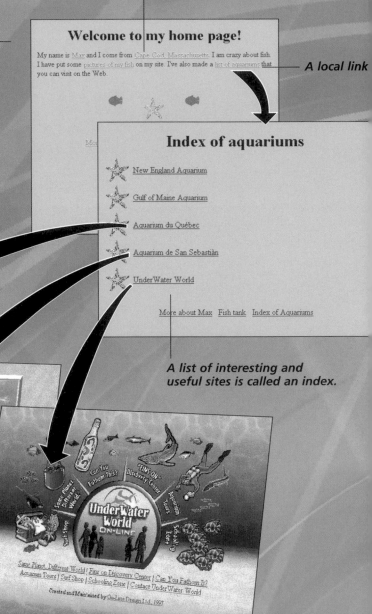

Creating a hyperlink

FrontPage® Express has tools for creating both local and global links. Here's what you do:

Creating a remote link

(1) Select the text you want to make into a hyperlink (see page 88 for selecting text).

(2) Click on *Insert*. A drop-down menu will appear. Click on *Hyperlink*.

(3) The Create Hyperlink window will appear with the *World Wide Web* property sheet selected.

(4) In the *URL* box, type the URL of the page to which you want to create a link and click on *OK*. FrontPage Express will create the hyperlink for you.

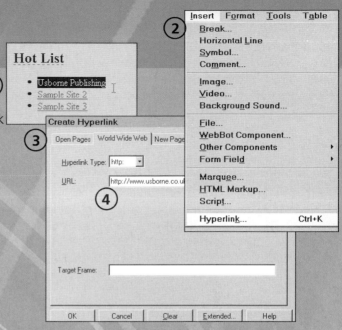

Creating a local link

To create a local link, first open both the pages you are linking. Follow stages 1 to 3 above, then:

(1) Select the *Open Pages* property sheet in the Create Hyperlink window. A list of the pages stored in your Web folder will appear in the Open Pages window.

(2) Click on the page you want the link to go to. Then click on *OK*.

(3) A warning will appear telling you that the file you are linking to may not be available to users of your web. As you will be uploading all your Web pages, this does not apply to you. Click on *Yes* and FrontPage Express will set up the hyperlink for you.

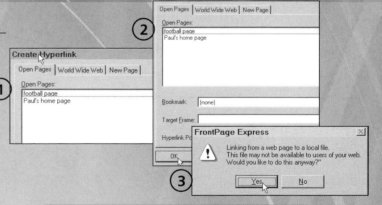

Site maintenance

The addresses of Web pages can change, and some pages are removed from the Web altogether. As a result, hyperlinks can become out-of-date or "invalid".

   Once your site is on the Internet, you should regularly check your links to other people's pages. Be sure to update or remove any invalid hyperlinks so that visitors to your site aren't disappointed or frustrated by them.

Including sounds

You can record sounds onto your computer and add them to your Web site. To do this, you may need some extra hardware and software.

Sound hardware

A computer uses a device called a sound card to capture sounds in digital format and play them back. All Macintosh computers and multimedia PCs contain sound cards. If you have another kind of computer, you may need to install one. You'll also need headphones or speakers to hear sounds coming from your computer.

Sound card

Speakers

Microphone

To record your own sounds, such as your voice, you will need a microphone that can be plugged into your computer. If you want to record something from a cassette or a CD, you will need a cable to connect your stereo to your computer.

Ready-made sounds

You may prefer to use ready-made sound clips on your site. You can find collections of sound clips on CD-ROM and on the Internet (see opposite).

Before you add a sound clip to your Web site, make sure that it is copyright-free (see page 39), or that you have permission from the person who created the sound.

Sound software

To create your own sound clips, you need a program that allows you to record and edit sound. You may already have such a program on your computer. The example shown below is Sound Recorder, a sound editing program that comes with Microsoft® Windows®. If you don't already have a suitable program, or you want a more advanced one, you can download one from the Internet (see pages 42-43 for information about downloading programs).

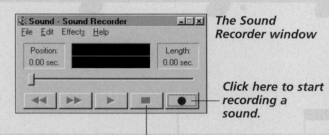

The Sound Recorder window

Click here to start recording a sound.

Click here to stop recording.

Sound file formats

There are several different types of sound files. The ones that are usually used on the Internet are: MP3, AU, MIDI, WAV and AIFF.

 MP3 files are the most widely used type of sound files on the Internet. They work on all types of computers.

 AU files work on all types of computers, but they sometimes sound a bit crackly.

MIDI files work on all types of computers and sound better than AU files.

 WAV is the Microsoft Windows audio format. Most browsers can play these files.

 AIFF is the Macintosh audio file format. Most browsers can play these files.

Create a sound clip

Use your sound editing program to record and save a sound in a suitable format. Your program may allow you to choose a recording quality. The higher the quality of the recording, the bigger the sound file will be.

Some sound programs enable you to add special effects or mix sounds together. For example, with Sound Recorder, you can add echoes to your sound or reverse it so that you hear everything backwards.

The Sound Selection dialog box from Sound Recorder.

Choose between CD, Radio or Telephone Quality.

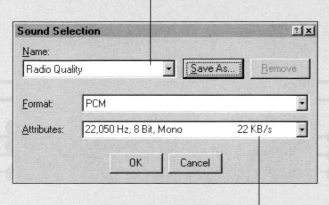

This tells you how many kilobytes (KB) of disk space one second of the selected sound quality requires.

Sound clips on the Web

 Sound files are usually very big files. A few seconds of speech can take up over 100 KB of disk space, even when it is recorded at low quality.

Not all Internet users want to spend time downloading sound clips, so it is better to create a hyperlink to a sound file rather than embed it directly in a Web page. Near the hyperlink, you should indicate how big the sound file is, how long it will play for, and what information it contains. This enables visitors to your site to decide whether or not they want to hear the sound clip. If they do, they can click on the hyperlink to download it.

Link to a sound file

You can create a link to a sound file using FrontPage® Express in the same way as you create a hyperlink. Place the sound file in your Web site folder, and then follow the instructions for creating hyperlinks on page 99.

When you follow a link to a sound file, a window containing a device called an audio player appears on screen. This plays sound files. Some audio players start automatically. With others, you have to click on a play button.

An audio player

Play/stop button

The slider bar moves across as the sound plays.

Sounds on the Internet

Here are a few address of places to download sound files and editing software:

Sound files:
www.sounddogs.com
www.soundamerica.com
www.earthstation1.com
cedar.alberni.net/absolute/hallosounds. html
www.webplaces.com/html/sounds.htm
Sound editing programs:
Cubase:**www.steinberg.net**
Cooledit:**www.syntrillium.com**
Mixman studio:**www.mixman. com**

Moving images

You can make your Web site more eye-catching by adding moving pictures, such as animations.

Animation

An animation is a moving image made from a sequence of pictures, known as frames. Each frame is slightly different from the previous one. When they are displayed in quick succession, the objects in the pictures appear to move.

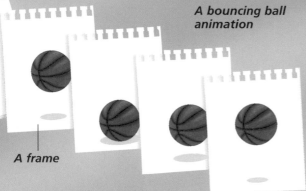

A bouncing ball animation

A frame

GIF animations

A GIF animation is produced from a series of GIF files. GIF animations are very popular on the Internet. They are easy to create and any browser that can show GIF files can play them.

Obtaining GIF animations

On the Internet, there are collections of GIF animations that you can use on your Web site for free. To find a GIF animation, perform a search for **animated GIF** or **GIF animation**.

You can embed GIF animations using Microsoft® FrontPage® Express in the same way as you embed ordinary images (see page 96).

This animation was saved from www.webpromotion.com.

Create your own GIF animations

To create your own GIF animations, you need an imaging program (see page 93) and a "GIF animation editor". This is a program that allows you to build up a sequence of GIF files (find out where to obtain one on page 103).

First, plan your animation on paper. Try to use as few frames as possible to form your animation, in order to keep the file size down. It is best not to use more than 12 frames.

Next, create the frames using your imaging program. Save each picture separately in GIF format. When saving animation frames, give each file a name that indicates where it comes in the sequence. This will be helpful when you build up your animation.

If these frames are shown in order, the clock's hand goes round.

clock1.gif   *clock2.gif*   *clock3.gif*   *clock4.gif*

Build up a GIF animation

Once you have created all the frames for your animation, use your GIF animation editor to bring them together into a single file.

Animation editors let you control the order in which the frames appear, and how many times over the animation will play.

Some programs let you specify other information, such as for how long each frame should appear.

Java™ applets

Another way to add animation and sound to a Web page is by embedding a Java™ applet.

Java applets can contain animation, sound and interactive features. This means you can change things on a Web page by clicking with your mouse. See the box below for sites where you can find ready-made applets to add to your site.

In this Java applet, moons whizz around a planet.

Including Java

Web sites that offer free Java applets usually include instructions for embedding them in a Web page.

To see a Java applet in operation, it is best to use Netscape® Navigator 4.03, Microsoft® Internet Explorer 4, or a later version of either of these browsers.

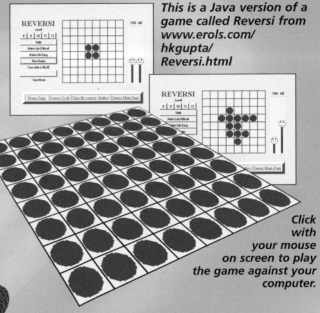

This is a Java version of a game called Reversi from www.erols.com/ hkgupta/ Reversi.html

Click with your mouse on screen to play the game against your computer.

Video

You can add a link to a video file using FrontPage Express in the same way as you add a link to a sound file (see page 101). However, video clips are more complicated to create, and they produce huge files that you or visitors to your site may have trouble downloading.

Useful sites for images

Animations:
www.barrysclipart.com
www.gifanimations.com
www.clipart.com
www.clipartconnection.com
Java™ applets:
www.javaboutique.internet.com
www.java.sun.com/applets
GIF animation editors:
For Microsoft® Windows®:
Webimage:
www.group42.com/webimage.htm
Ulead® GIF Animator™: **www.ulead.com**
For Macintosh computers:
GIF builder:
www.pascal.com/mirrors/gifbuilder

Viewing pages

Before you put your Web pages onto the Internet, you should open them in your browser to see how they will look online. This will also allow you to check that all the hyperlinks work and view any animations on your pages in action.

Opening your Web pages

① Open your browser window. Open the *File* menu and select *Open*.

② An Open window will appear. Click on the *Browse* button.

③ An Explorer window will appear. Select your home page file from the hard drive.

④ An Open window will appear. Click on the *OK* button.

⑤ Your home page will appear in the browser window.

Your Web site should look and function the same way through your browser offline as it will online. All the local and remote links you have included should be working, so click on them to test that they are active.

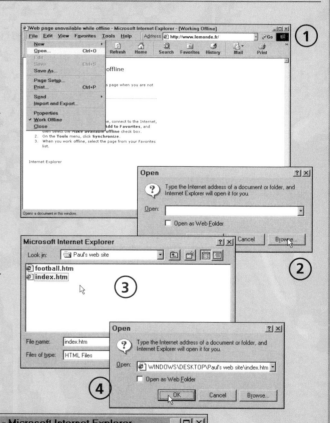

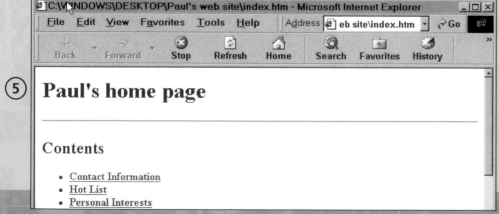

Ready for the Internet?

Here are some of the things you should do before you put your site on the Internet.

Accuracy and efficiency

You should check your site by carefully rereading each page through your browser. Ensure that all the information on your site is correct and that there are enough local links to enable visitors to find their way around easily (see page 99).

It isn't easy for you to see your site from a visitor's point of view. Things that appear obvious to you, such as where to find a particular piece of information, may not be obvious to others. If possible, ask a friend to explore your site for you. They may be able to suggest some improvements.

Checklist for a Web site

Check your spelling and make sure any facts and figures are correct.

Make sure all the local links work properly. To do this, click on each one to see whether it lets you jump to the right page.

Make sure you have specified the size of any large files people might want to download.

Ensure the most important information on a particular page can be seen without the use of the scroll bars.

If you have used animations or pictures from other Web pages, make sure you have permission to use them. See page 39 for information about copyright.

Filing system

You should store all the files for your Web site in one folder on your computer's hard disk (for information about saving files, see page 86). If there are a lot of files, you may want to create some subdirectories within your site's main directory. If you move a file, remember to update the relevant links on your Web pages so that browsers can still locate it. If a browser can't locate a picture file, it displays an icon instead.

Netscape shows this icon when it can't find a picture file.

Use different equipment

A Web page may appear slightly different when it is looked at using a different computer, browser, operating system or type of Internet connection. If possible, try out your Web site on a variety of different machines to check that it looks acceptable on all of them.

Finishing touches

Include the date you finished your site so that visitors know how up-to-date it is.

Finally, make extra copies of all your Web site files. That way, if anything happens to the computer to which you transfer your site, you won't have lost all your hard work.

Providing Web space

Web sites are stored on powerful computers called servers or hosts. Before people can visit your site, you will have to transfer it to a Web server. Unless you have your own server, you will need to rent space on someone else's. A company that rents out space on Web servers is known as a hosting company.

A server

Internet service providers

The fastest way to get your site online is using an ISP (see pages 12-13). The account you set up with your current ISP may include free Web space. If your existing ISP does not offer you free Web space, or if the hosting service they provide doesn't suit you, you may want to open an account with a different ISP to host your site. You can have accounts with as many different ISPs as you like.

Other Web host providers

Some Web host providers charge a monthly fee for their services. These companies offer extra benefits, such as security features for doing business on the Web. Unless you are setting up a business, you are unlikely to need to use one of these hosts.

Making choices

You can find the addresses of Internet service providers and other Web host providers in Internet magazines or on the Web. Each company offers a slightly different service.

Here are some questions that you might like to ask before you choose a company to host your Web site:

How fast will my site download?
Find out how powerful the servers are, and how they are linked to the Internet. The more powerful the server, the quicker your pages will download.

When two or more computers are connected, a channel for exchanging information is formed. The maximum amount of data a channel can transfer is known as its "bandwidth capability".

Most hosting companies use fibre optic cables to connect their servers to the Internet. There are four types of fibre optic cable. T1 cables have a bandwidth capability of up to 1.5 megabits of data per second (Mbps), T2 cables have a bandwidth capability of up to 6.3 Mbps, T3 cables have a bandwidth capability of up to 44 Mbps and ATM cables have a bandwidth capability of over 100 Mbps. Check which cables your host is using, as it will affect the speed at which your Web pages download.

It's a good idea to visit a hosting company's Web site to see how quickly their own pages download. If they can't deliver their own pages quickly, they are unlikely to be able to offer you a better service.

The newest development to affect download speed is Digital Subscriber Lines (DSL). These are very fast Internet connections which can download data at a speed of up to 512 Kbps using DSL adaptors and existing telephone lines. DSL technology is still fairly new, but it should be widely available in the near future.

How much space will you provide?

Most ISPs offer customers free Internet space to store their site, but the amount they offer varies enormously. If your site is fairly small this won't be a problem, but if you are planning to put a lot of pictures on it, then you should make sure that the ISP you choose offers enough space to store all the information on your pages.

Internet magazines run regular summaries of the benefits of different ISPs and the amount of hosting space they offer. It is worth looking at these before you decide who you want to host your site.

Do you provide technical support?

You may need advice on how to transfer your site to the Web and how to maintain it. Find out if a company provides support for its customers and whether this is done by telephone or by e-mail. Make sure support will be available at the times of day when you are most likely to need it.

What extra services do you offer?

Depending on the content of your Web site, you may require some extra services. For example, if you intend to use your site to sell things, you will need a hosting company that can make it safe for you to use your site to collect private information such as credit card details and telephone numbers.

You may expect a lot of the people that will use your site to access the Internet through fast lines, such as DSL lines. If so, make sure the host you choose has a compatible Internet connection.

Make sure a hosting company can provide all the extra services you may require.

Getting ready to upload

If you are planning to use a new ISP to host your site, you will need to set up an account with them first (see pages 12-17 for information about setting up an account with an ISP).

Next, you will need to get a Web address (URL) for your site from your chosen host. This is a straightforward process, but it varies for different hosts. You may find that your Web space and address were allocated when you set up your original account. Alternatively, you may need to fill out a set of forms online before your host will allocate any space and give you an address.

Visit your host server's home page. There should be a local link you can click on which will take you through the procedure for getting your Web space. If the link is not immediately obvious, go to your server's help pages, which should include information on how to register for Web space.

Checklist

You need the following information to upload your site:
1. Your user name.
2. Your password.
3. The "host" name (your server's URL).
4. Your URL.

You are now ready to put your site on the Internet. For uploading instructions, turn to page 108.

Uploading your site

This section shows you how to transfer your Web site files onto your hosting company's server. Copying files from your computer onto another computer on the Internet is called uploading. The fastest way to upload files is by using a method called File Transfer Protocol (FTP).

FTP clients

To transfer files by FTP, you need a program called an FTP client. The one shown on these pages is called WS_FTP®.

When you open an FTP client, you will see a window divided into two parts, similar to the one shown below. The left part displays a list of the files that are stored on your computer, called the local computer. The right part is used to display the files that are stored on other computers, known as remote computers.

The first time you open your FTP client, the right part of the window will be blank. This is because your computer is not yet connected to a remote computer.

Preparations

In order to upload your Web site, you have to connect your computer to your hosting company's server. To instruct your FTP client to do this, you need to enter some information, such as the server's address, into a dialog box.

With WS_FTP, this dialog box appears each time you start the program. Your hosting company will tell you exactly what information you need to enter in order to connect to their server (see page 107).

Connecting

Once you have given your FTP client this information, you are ready to connect your computer to the hosting company's server.

Connect to the Internet in the usual way. Then click on the Connect button in your FTP client. When your FTP client has connected to the server, the files that are stored on the server will appear on the right side of the window.

A window from an FTP client called WS_FTP

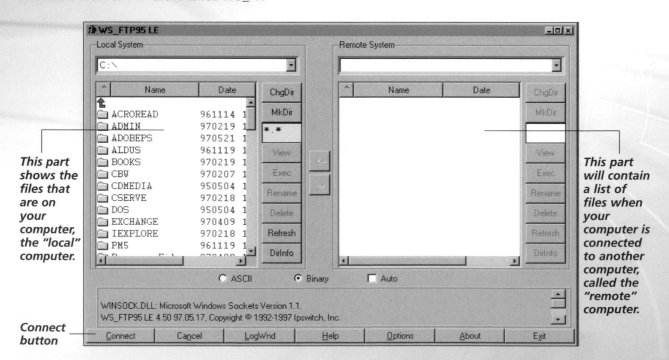

This part shows the files that are on your computer, the "local" computer.

Connect button

This part will contain a list of files when your computer is connected to another computer, called the "remote" computer.

Transferring files

First, use the left part of your FTP client's window to locate your Web site files on your computer's hard disk. You can open a directory or folder by double-clicking on its icon.

Next use the right part of the window to open the directory on the server where you are going to store your Web site. Your hosting company will tell you which directory you should use.

To transfer a file, select its file name with your mouse and click on the button which points to the right.

When a file has been successfully transferred to the server, its file name will appear in the right part of the window.

Transferring files with WS_FTP

Use this button to upload files.

As soon as you have finished transferring a file, anyone with access to the Internet can look at it as a Web page. Typing in your URL will take them to your default or index page (see page 86). From there, they can use the links to work their way around your site.

After uploading

Publicizing your site
To enable other Internet users to find your site, you should tell a selection of search engines about it (see pages 44-49).

To do this, go to a search engine's home page and look for a hyperlink called Add URL or something similar. Click on this link to download a registration form. A search engine will use the information you enter onto its form to find and classify your site.

To avoid repeating this process many times, you can use a service that automatically submits the details of your site to several search services.

Hundreds of sites are added to the Internet every day. A search engine won't be able to visit your site immediately. You may have to wait several weeks after registration for your site to appear in a search engine's directory.

Updating your site
To update your Web site, you have to change the original files that are stored on your computer. When you are happy with the changes, transfer the new versions of the files to the server. Your FTP client will use these to replace the old versions, provided they have the same file names.

FTP clients on the Internet

For Microsoft® Windows®:
WS_FTP®: **www.ipswitch.com**
CuteFTP: **www.cuteftp.com**
Ace FTP: **www.visicommedia.com**

For Macintosh computers:
Fetch: **www.dartmouth.edu/pages/ softdev**

Future developments

The Internet is developing all the time. More and more people are getting connected to it and companies are creating products that make it easier to use. The most popular Internet facilities, such as e-mail and the World Wide Web, may not change much in the near future, but it will almost certainly become quicker, easier and less expensive to connect to them.

High-speed connections

Most people connecting to the Internet at home currently use a modem connected to the telephone network. However, a standard 56K modem downloads Web pages relatively slowly, especially if they have a lot of information in the form of pictures, sound or video files. Faster connections are now becoming available, and could revolutionize the way we use the Internet.

The same technology which brings you cable TV can also offer high-speed Internet access. Your Internet connection is available all the time – you don't have to wait for your modem to dial your ISP each time you connect. A cable modem can download data at around 512K, almost ten times as fast as a telephone modem.

However, since a number of households share use of the same cable, some users find their connection is slower when a lot of people are using the service at once. The service is still fairly expensive, and is not available everywhere.

Fibre optic cables can transmit large amounts of data at high speed.

A cable modem

DSL connection

DSL, or Digital Subscriber Line, uses existing telephone lines to transfer data at high speeds, generally around ten times as fast as a 56K modem. Like cable connections, DSL Internet connections are permanently available, so it is easy to send messages or check facts quickly.

However, you have to pay a fairly high monthly charge for use of the service, and since you are connected all the time, you are more at risk from hackers. It is a good idea to install a "personal firewall" – software which protects you from people having unauthorized access to your computer.

Internet entertainment

When high-speed access becomes more widespread, there will be a range of services available to take advantage of it. You might select and download a film in minutes, just as you would choose a video – but with the Internet you could choose from a huge range of titles without even leaving home. There are also plans to show major sporting events as Webcasts (see page 59). With a standard 56K modem connection, picture download speed and quality are rarely high enough to show sports matches clearly, but they will be much better through a high-speed connection.

It will be possible to watch major sports matches, such as this European Cup game between France and Portugal, as Webcasts.

Wireless connections

A number of leading telecommunications and software companies are working together to develop wireless Internet connections, using radio waves. This technology is called Bluetooth™, and can be incorporated in desktop and laptop computers, PDAs and mobile phones, making it easy to communicate and connect to the Internet wherever you are.

What is more, different devices will be able to connect to each other automatically. For example, when you go to work, your laptop and mobile phone will automatically connect with your office computer network and download the addresses and telephone numbers you need at work.

Internet around the home

Several major software companies are working on connecting domestic appliances, such as refrigerators and microwave ovens, to the Internet. An Internet-connected microwave, for example, could download recipes and cooking instructions from the Internet, while a refrigerator could order fresh ingredients from an online supermarket. Even a garden sprinkler could download weather information to tell it when to water the lawn.

You could also use the Internet to keep an eye on your home while you are away, or to let a friend or relative into the house while you are on holiday.

A panel in the door of this refrigerator can display recipe pages from the Internet.

Internet on the road

The French car manufacturer Citroën has developed a car with a voice-controlled computer replacing the in-car entertainment system. As well as playing radio and CDs, it incorporates a navigation system, a mobile phone and e-mail. The computer can download traffic and weather reports, and although it is not yet able to browse the Web, this should soon be possible.

This car has a voice-activated computer which can send and receive e-mail and download travel information.

Internet pets

Sony®'s robot dog, Aibo, was a huge success when it was first sold in a limited edition in Japan and the USA. Aibo "learns" behaviour patterns over time, and responds to praise or scolding from its owners. Its behaviour can also be programmed using special software.

Sony's Aibo

In time, new tricks and behaviour patterns could be downloaded via the Internet.

Find out more

You can read more about some of the developments on these pages at:

DSL connection:
www.btopenworld.com

Wireless connections:
www.bluetooth.com

Internet-linked appliances:
www.sun.com/consumer-embedded/cover/ces

Citroën "Windows" car:
www.citroen.com/us/index.html
(choose *Search* and type *Citroen Xsara Windows CE*)

Sony® Aibo:
www.world.sony.com/aibo

Mobile Internet

One of the most exciting developments in the way we use the Internet is that we can now connect on the move, using PDAs (Personal Digital Assistants) or mobile phones. These are also called WAP phones, after the computer language, Wireless Application Protocol, which is used to send data to them.

PDAs

Some PDAs are like pocket-size laptop computers, with tiny keyboards and LCD (liquid crystal display) screens, which show information in grey and green only. Some models even incorporate a mobile phone, which they can use to connect to the Internet, while others connect via a separate mobile phone or a modem attachment.

This PDA has a small keyboard attached.

Other kinds of PDAs don't have a keyboard. You use a touch-sensitive screen and a special pen called a"stylus" to enter data. These PDAs, too, connect to the Internet via a mobile phone or modem. They can have LCD or colour screens, and use specially adapted versions of PC applications such as Microsoft® Windows®, Outlook® Express and Internet Explorer.

Keeping it small

In order to keep PDAs small and lightweight, software manufacturers have devised versions of their programs that can run without needing a large amount of power, and can be displayed on a small screen. To browse the World Wide Web, for example, PDAs use a special kind of browser called a microbrowser, which can show the information on a Web page on a much smaller screen than an ordinary PC.

This PDA has a larger screen and a stylus for entering data.

Mobile phones

Mobile phones are even more convenient to carry around than PDAs, and they can incorporate a modem to connect to the Internet. They are also much less expensive than a PDA or a PC. However, they only have a tiny screen, and are not powerful enough to download lots of complicated data.

Mobile phones can often be used to send text messages, similar to e-mail. Numbers on the keypad are used to type letters of the alphabet. Some phones use a system called "predictive text input" to guess the ending of a word when you start to type it, and this can make typing faster and easier. Many mobile phones can use SMS (Short Messaging System) to send messages of up to 160 characters (the equivalent of four lines in this paragraph). However, SMS messages can only be sent to other SMS-equipped phones.

MP3 via mobile

You can now have a mobile phone that also works as a portable MP3 player (see page 59). The phones have enough memory for around half an hour's worth of music. You can download copyright-free tracks from MP3 sites on the Internet, or go to special "docking stations" in music stores, and download tracks directly to the phone.

This phone can play MP3 tracks.

Find out more

You can read more about some of the products on this page at:

PDAs:
www.psion.com/revo
www.palm.com
www.casio.com/mobileinformation

MP3 phones:
www.samsungelectronics.com/mobile/products

WAP

Some phones can connect to the Internet and download material in "WAP format". Wireless Application Protocol is a computer language used to present information very simply, in black and white and usually as plain text, so that it can easily be downloaded and displayed on a very small screen. It is used to create WAP sites, which are like Web sites that can be downloaded to WAP-enabled phones.

There are not nearly as many WAP sites as there are Web sites, but more are being created all the time. The first WAP sites were mainly information sites such as news, stock market information, weather and traffic reports, but more commercial sites are being developed.

You can use a WAP phone to keep up with the latest news.

You can now manage your bank account with a WAP phone, check cinema listings and book tickets, buy books and CDs and even plan a holiday. You can also send and receive e-mail, and check e-mail you receive at another e-mail address, such as your address at work or at home.

How do I get connected?

To use WAP services, you'll need to have a WAP-enabled mobile phone. The majority of new mobile phones are WAP-enabled, but they are generally more expensive to buy and to use than standard mobile phones. You will also need to set up an account with an ISP. Usually, your account will be set up for you when you buy your phone.

Connection speed

Connection speed for WAP phones is increasing all the time. Fast, reliable "third-generation" mobile connections, which will be available in 2002, will offer speeds of up to 384K, making it possible to download colour, images, sound and video.

This is a WAP phone.

Personalized service

When you use a company's services on the Internet, either via a PC or via a WAP phone, they will be able to gather information about you which can help them to serve you in the future. For example, if you enjoy a particular kind of holiday, a travel agent could let you know instantly about a special deal.

Some mobile phones incorporate GPS (Global Positioning System), a technology which uses satellite to pinpoint exactly where you are anywhere in the world, within 20 metres.

In future, this could be used by companies to send you information related to your position, such as traffic reports for your immediate area or route, or details of restaurants in the neighbourhood.

WAP future

WAP technology is developing incredibly fast. Around twice as many people in the world have a mobile phone as have a PC, so WAP has the potential to become the most popular way of connecting to the Internet. The services available today are fairly limited, but we can expect to see huge advances in the next year or two.

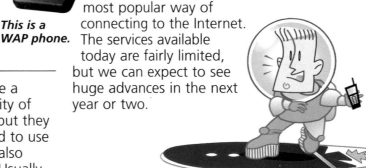

WAP and WAP phones

You can find out more about WAP in general at: **www.wapforum.org**

You can also find lots of information on the following manufacturers' Web sites:
gx-2.net/wwow/overview.html
www.nokia.com/wap/index.html
www.ericsson.com/WAP

Problems and solutions

Whether you are using your own computer at home, or you are part of a large business network, you will occasionally have problems connecting to or using the Internet. This section looks at some common problems, and what you can do about them.

What if I can't connect at all?

Sometimes you may have difficulty connecting to the Internet. This often happens when a lot of people are trying to go online at the same time and your ISP is busy. Your Dial-up Connection window may say "Unable to establish a connection".

If this happens, your Internet connection software may try again automatically, or you may have to click on the *Connect* button to try again. Try once or twice more, and if this doesn't work, try again later. Ask your ISP when its busiest periods are, and try and avoid them. If you often have difficulty connecting, you may want to change your ISP.

A Dial-up Connection window will tell you if you have a problem connecting to the Internet.

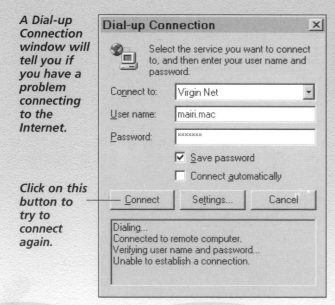

Click on this button to try to connect again.

Incorrect password If you have to type in a password, make sure that you type it correctly. Sometimes the system which accepts your password is "case sensitive", meaning that you have to use capital letters and small letters in the same places each time.

Authentication failed You may get an error message saying that your "authentication" has failed. When you try to connect, your modem sends a signal to your ISP's server. This signal, known as a handshake, tells the server who you are and confirms that you have permission to use it to connect to the Internet.

If your authentication has failed, it means your handshake has not been recognized. There may be a problem with your ISP's server, or you may not have set up your connection software properly. Call your ISP's helpline and ask for advice.

What if I can't pick up my e-mail?

If you are expecting e-mail and none has arrived, there may be a number of explanations.

Mail server fault There could be a problem with your ISP's e-mail server. If you still have access to the Web, you may be able to check this online: go to your ISP's home page, and look for a link to "Member services" or "Service announcements". If your ISP hasn't reported any faults, the problem may be with the sender's ISP. Usually ISPs are able to correct faults within a day or so.

Wrong address The person who is trying to contact you may simply have got your address wrong. Remember, it is important to get e-mail addresses exactly right, or a message will not be delivered.

What if I get a virus via e-mail?

 If you suspect that an e-mail contains a virus, delete it immediately without opening it. Make sure that you also delete it from your Deleted Items folder. If you get a virus warning via e-mail and you are not sure whether it is a hoax or not (see page 28), you could look for hoaxes of that name on a virus information Web site such as the F Secure site (**www.datafellows.com/virus-info/hoax**).

If you do get a real virus via e-mail, contact your ISP and ask their advice.

Problems on the World Wide Web

Web connections are becoming better and more reliable all the time, but problems can still occur. The most common problems are: missing Web pages, pages with faults and Internet congestion (when a lot of people are using the Internet at once).

 Wrong address You may type in a URL and get a message saying "The page cannot be displayed" or "Unable to locate the server" or "HTTP 404 – File not found". This may be a temporary connection problem. Try clicking on the *Refresh* button first of all. If this does not work, it could be because you typed the URL incorrectly – try typing again, and take care with abbreviations such as .com or .org.

If you typed in a fairly long address such as **moma.e-cards.org/catalogue**, you could try "drilling down". This means taking away a part of the address after a slash (/) to try to get to another page on the same Web site.

 Page unavailable If you still have no luck, the page may be unavailable because of problems with its host server, and you may be able to connect to it another time.

 Page removed The page may have been taken off the Web altogether. Some sites put up messages when pages are removed, but not all do, and you may have to find what you are looking for on another site.

 Change of address Sometimes Web sites change their URLs. Usually when this happens, you will find a message on the site of the original URL, giving you the new one. If the site was one of your Favorites (see page 38), you should change its URL using the *Organize Favorites...* command. Sometimes you will be redirected to the new site automatically, or you may have to click on the new URL to go to the new site.

 Errors on the page The page may only partly download, and you may see a message saying that there are errors. Try clicking on the *Refresh* button.

Too slow

 If Web pages take a long time to download, it can be very frustrating – and expensive, if you are paying for your time online.

 Server problems There may be a temporary problem with the Web site's host server. Try clicking on the *Refresh* button first of all. The problem may also be Internet congestion in general. Try connecting to the site later, when the Internet is likely to be less busy.

Slow computer or modem If you generally find that Web pages take a very long time to download, it may be that your computer is not very powerful or you don't have a high-speed modem. You might want to consider replacing one or the other.

With millions of people using the Internet, there are bound to be those who misuse it. However, there are lots of precautions you can take that will ensure the Internet is a safe place to surf.

E-mail

Don't give your e-mail address out to strangers. You wouldn't give your home address out to a complete stranger, so why should your e-mail address be any different?

Be careful who you give your e-mail address to. Companies often ask you to fill out a form with your e-mail address on when you buy their products or download software. Look for a box to tick, stating that you don't want to receive any information from the company, otherwise you may end up receiving annoying spam (see page 28).

Personal details

Many Web sites, especially shopping sites, ask you to fill in forms giving information including your name, address, e-mail address and telephone number, so that they can contact you to tell you about special offers. You should only ever give your details to well-known and well-established companies.

Most reliable Internet companies take good care of your details – check to see whether the site has a "privacy policy" which tells you that any personal details you give will not be misused or passed on to anyone else.

Meeting up

Someone you chat to online may suggest meeting up in real life. This is generally a bad idea. Remember that it is easy for people online to pretend to be somebody they aren't. If you can't see someone or hear their voice, you have no idea whether they are male or female, eight years old or 80. To avoid disappointments or even danger, it's best to keep online friendships strictly online.

Viruses

Your computer can catch a virus over the Internet if you copy files from an infected computer, or open an infected e-mail attachment. Viruses spread very fast over the Internet. The "I Love You" virus, for example, was released on May 4th, 2000 and had become a global problem within 24 hours. It is now estimated to have caused up to $15 billion worth of damage to businesses worldwide.

Make sure that you have anti-virus software installed on your computer. For more information about viruses, see page 16.

Hackers

Hackers are people who access computer systems without permission. They can link up their own computers to networks, and open private files. By changing the information in these files, they may be able to steal money or goods.

If your computer is on a network and you have private information stored on it, remember that other people can very easily access your files.

If you are using a computer at home, it is unlikely that people can access your files.

Internet potatoes

Some Internet facilities, such as games and IRC, can become very addictive. If you are paying for the time you spend online this can prove very expensive. In addition, using a computer for any purpose for long periods of time can damage your health.

It's essential to take a ten minute break every hour that you use a computer, to rest your eyes and other parts of your body.

There's more to life than surfing the Internet. So make sure you don't become an Internet potato and end up at the receiving end of a common Internet insult... GAL, which means Get A Life!

Offensive material

People are free to publish whatever they like on the Internet. So, as well as interesting things, there's also unpleasant, unsuitable and dangerous information out there. Be careful to avoid anything you don't want to look at. Both Microsoft® Internet Explorer and Netscape® Navigator can be adjusted to block access to certain sites.

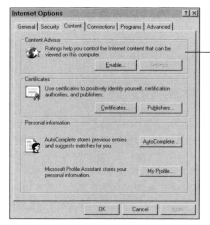

The Internet Options Content window in Internet Explorer can be opened from the menu bar: go to View – Internet Options – Content. Netscape Navigator has a similar feature which can be opened from the menu bar: go to Help – Netwatch.

Filters are programs which check and restrict the information you can download from the Internet. You can change what these programs restrict to suit your own needs.

If you are in a chat room and somebody says something which makes you feel uncomfortable, don't respond. If they persist, let the monitor of the chat room, or the online service providing the chat room, know about it.

A filter program called Net Nanny®

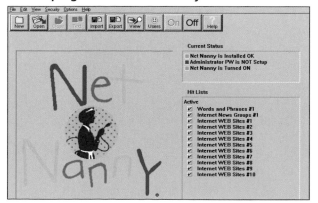

Buying online

If you decide to buy anything over the Internet, make sure that the site you are buying from is secure before you give your financial details. A secure Web site will translate your details into code so that they can't be used by anyone else.

Both Microsoft Internet Explorer and Netscape Navigator show a closed padlock in the browser window when a site is secure.

Internet fraud is a controversial issue, but though it is possible to commit a crime online, it is no easier than it is in the real world, and criminals are far easier to trace.

For more information about safe shopping online, see page 63.

If a site is secure, Internet Explorer shows this padlock at the bottom of the browser window.

Software protection

Spam filtering software:
www.spamkiller.com
www.scotdemon.co.uk/spam-filter.html

Virus information:
www.f-secure.com/virus-info

Anti-virus software:
Norton AntiVirus™: **www.symantec.com**
Dr Solomon's Virex®:**www.drsolomon.com/home/home.cfm**
McAfee VirusScan®: **www.mcafee.com**

Filter programs:
Cyber Patrol®:
www.cyberpatrol.com
Net Nanny®:
www.netnanny.com

Glossary

Here's a list of some of the Internet words you may come across, either in this book or elsewhere, with their meanings. The meanings given in this list are specific to the Internet. Some of the words have different meanings in other contexts.

Any word which appears in *italic* type is defined elsewhere in the glossary.

access provider see *Internet Access Provider*.

acronym A word made up of the first letters of words in a phrase, such as *WYSIWYG*.

ActiveX® A Microsoft® product for including *multimedia* effects on *Web pages*.

address The location of a *Web page* on the *Internet*.

address book A part of your e-mail program where you can store other people's *e-mail* addresses.

address box The box in your *browser* window where you type a *URL*, or where a *URL* is displayed.

ADSL see *DSL*.

AIM see *Instant messaging*.

alphaware Very early trial versions of software.

animation A moving image made by showing a series of pictures in quick succession.

anti-virus software Software which protects your computer from *viruses*.

applet A small program produced with the programming language *Java*, which can be inserted in a *Web page*.

application A program which enables your computer to create documents or perform tasks.

archive 1. The place on an *Internet host* where files are stored. 2. A *file* which contains a group of *compressed files*.

attachment A *file*, such as a picture file or *animation*, sent with an *e-mail*.

avatar A moveable on-screen character which represents a computer user in a *virtual world*.

back-up A copy of a computer program or document.

backbone An important link between large *servers* on the *Internet*, which carries a lot of information at high speeds.

bandwidth A measurement of the amount of *data* that can flow through a link between computers. It is usually measured in *bits* per second (*bps*).

banner A piece of advertising across the top of a *Web page*.

BCC (blind carbon copy) A copy of an *e-mail* in which the person receiving the copy can't see who else the message has been sent to.

betaware Trial versions of software, more fully developed than *alphaware*.

bit The smallest unit of computer *data*.

body The main part of an *e-mail*.

bookmark Netscape® Navigator's way of storing a *URL* so that you can visit the *Web site* again quickly and easily.

Boolean query or **Boolean search** A way of refining a *search engine* search using special *operators*.

bounce When *e-mail* can't be delivered to its destination and is returned.

bps (bits per second) The basic measurement of how fast *data* is transferred.

broadband High-speed *data* transfer between computers.

browser A program used to find and display documents stored on the *Web*.

browsing Exploring the *Web*. See *surfing*.

bug A problem in a computer program which prevents it from working properly.

byte A unit of eight *bits*.

cable modem A very high speed *modem* which uses the cable network (used for cable television) instead of telephone lines.

cache The part of a computer's memory where *Web pages* that have been *downloaded* are temporarily stored.

case-sensitive A system which recognizes the difference between capital letters and small letters.

CC (carbon copy) A copy of an *e-mail* to let someone know what you are saying to someone else.

chat Having a conversation with other *Internet* users by typing questions and answers.

chat room A *Web site* where a number of *Internet* users can *chat* at once.

client A computer which uses the services of a *host* or *server* computer.

clip art Pictures, usually *copyright*-free, which can be used to illustrate documents.

community A *Web site* which encourages visitors to share their views.

compression Making a smaller version of a *file*, so that it takes less space in a computer's memory, and less time to *download*.

cookie A *file* on your computer's hard disk which is used by *Web sites* to store information about you, such as when you last visited the site and which pages you *downloaded*.

copyright The legal obligation to obtain permission to reproduce text, music or images.

counter A device on a *Web page* which shows how often the page has been visited.

country code The part of an *address* which shows where an organization is based.

crash A sudden failure in a computer system.

cyberspace The imaginary space that you travel around in when you use the *Internet*.

data Information processed by a computer.

decompression Extracting a full-size *file* from a *compressed file*.

default 1. The automatic setting in an *application*, before you make any changes. 2. Often, the *HTML* name for a *home page*.

dial-up Using a *modem* and the telephone network to connect to the *Internet*.

digicam see *digital camera*.

digital Information recorded as a number code that can be read and processed by computers.

digital camera A camera that stores pictures as *digital data* that can be processed by a computer.

digital signature A short piece of *encrypted* text at the end of a document which can be used to identify the document sender.

digitize To translate information into number code that can be processed by computers.

directory A *search engine* which sorts *Web sites* into categories.

DNS (Domain Name Service) The system of giving organizations on the *Internet* names which are unique to them and can be recognized by other *Internet* users.

domain name The part of an *address* which gives information about an organization, what kind of organization it is or where it is based.

down A computer or system which is not working.

download To copy a *Web page* or a program from a computer on the *Internet* to your own computer.

dpi (dots per inch) A measure of *resolution*.

drilling down Taking away parts of a *URL* in order to go to other pages on the same *Web site*.

DSL (Digital Subscriber Line) A high-speed *Internet* connection via ordinary telephone lines.

e-mail (electronic mail) A way of sending messages via the *Internet* from one user to another.

embed To insert an image or a file in a *Web page* or other computer document.

emoticon see *smiley*.

encryption Translating information, such as financial information, into code to keep it secure.

expansion card A device, such as a sound card, that gives a computer extra features.

FAQ (Frequently Asked Questions) A *Web page* or a document used by *mailing lists* or *newsgroups* that lists the answers to questions often asked by new visitors or new members.

favorite Internet Explorer's equivalent of *bookmarks* – a way of storing a *URL* so that you can visit the *Web site* again another time.

file Anything stored on a computer, such as a document, an image or a program.

file format The way a program stores information.

filter A program that checks *Web pages* or incoming *e-mail*, and blocks out unwanted or undesirable content.

firewall A security system used to prevent unauthorized users from gaining access to a *network*, such as a company network.

flame An angry or rude *e-mail* or message sent to a *newsgroup*.

Flash™ A highly-developed kind of *animation* used on *Web sites*.

follow-up A message sent to a *newsgroup* commenting on a previously *posted* message.

forum A discussion area on a *Web site*.

frame One of a series of images which make up an *animation*.

freeware Programs which can be *downloaded* and used free of charge.

FTP (File Transfer Protocol) A language used to transfer *files* over the *Internet*.

GIF An image *file format* often used for pictures on the *Web*.

GIF animation A type of *GIF* used for *animation* sequences.

guestbook A device that allows visitors to a *Web site* to leave their names and comments.

hacker Someone who gains unauthorized access to a computer or network, and may change or destroy information stored there.

header The part of an *e-mail* containing the sender's name, recipient's name, the date and message subject.

hit 1. A page found by a *search engine* which contains the *keywords* of the original *query*. 2. A visit to a *Web site*. The number of hits can be recorded using a *counter*.

home page 1. The first page which *downloads* when you open your *browser*. 2. The first page which *downloads* when you visit a *Web site*, or the main page from which you can go to other pages.

host 1. A computer connected to the *Internet* which can give out information to other users. 2. An organization which runs a *Web site* for another organization or individual.

Hotmail® A popular *e-mail* service, which can be accessed from any computer via the *Web*.

HTML (HyperText Mark-up Language) The computer code used to create *Web pages*.

HTML editor see *Web editor*.

HTTP (HyperText Transfer Protocol) The language computers use to transfer *Web* pages across the *Internet*.

hub A *Web site* containing news or other information which people refer to frequently.

hyperlink A piece of text or a picture that acts as a link from one *Web page* to another.

hypertext A word or group of words which is a *hyperlink*.

icon A symbol representing an *application*, or a larger object such as a picture or sound *file* on a *Web page*.

index A *search engine* that lists millions of *Web sites*, and selects Web sites by matching *keywords*.

instant messaging A way of *chatting* to friends online.

intellectual property see *copyright*.

interactive A *Web site*, or part of a *Web site*, which the user can respond to or change.

Internet The vast computer *network* made by linking computers together around the world.

Internet Access Provider or **Internet Service Provider** A company which offers access to the *Internet*.

InterNIC (Internet Network Information Center) An organization in the US that gives out *domain names* and regulates their use.

intranet A *network* of computers within an organization, which can only be accessed by people in that organization.

invalid A *hyperlink* or *URL* which doesn't work.

IP (Internet Protocol) The language which allows computers to recognize each other over the *Internet*.

IRC (Internet Relay Chat) A popular *chat* system.

ISDN (Integrated Services Digital Network) A type of line which can transfer information between computers about twice as fast as a standard 56*K modem*.

ISP see *Internet Service Provider*.

Java™ A programming language which can be read by all *platforms*, used to add *animations* and *interactive* features to *Web pages*.

JPEG An image *file format* often used for photographs on the *Web*.

K or **Kbps** Thousand bits per second, used as a measure of connection speed, as in "56K modem".

KB or **kilobyte** Approximately 1,000 *bytes*.

keyword 1. A word which describes a document's content. 2. A word used in a *search engine query*. 3. A word you type into the *address box* in AOL to go to another part of the service, such as Entertainment.

LAN (Local Area Network) A *network* of computers within an organization which is also connected to the *Internet*.

link 1. A connection between computers. 2. A *hyperlink*.

log in or **log on** To connect to a computer, to a *network*, to an *online service* or to the *Internet*.

lurking Reading the messages in a *chat room* or a *newsgroup* without sending any yourself.

mailbox The place where an *online service* or *ISP* stores new *e-mail* for you.

mailing list A discussion group where messages are sent to the group members via *e-mail*.

mail server A computer that handles *e-mail*.

MB or **megabyte** About one million *bytes*.

meta tag A tag that helps a *search engine* to classify a *Web page*.

MIDI (Musical Instrument Digital Interface) A way of transferring *data* between computers and electronic musical instruments.

MIME (Multi-purpose Internet Mail Extensions) The language used to transfer *e-mail attachments* via the *Internet*.

modem A device used to send and receive computer *data* across the telephone network.

MPEG A *file format* used for audio and video clips on the *Web*.

MP3 A *file format* used for music clips which takes up very little computer memory without losing much sound quality.

multimedia Presenting information in various formats, which might include text, pictures, sound and video.

Net see *Internet*.

Netiquette The proper way to behave when using the *Internet*.

network A group of computers, *linked* so that they can share information and equipment.

newbie A new *Internet* user or a new member of a *newsgroup*.

newsgroup A place on the *Internet* where people with the same interests can *post* messages and see other people's responses.

offline Not connected to the *Internet*.

online Connected to the *Internet*.

online service A company that gives you access to its own private *network* as well as to the *Internet*.

operator A word or symbol which helps a *search engine* to make a search more specific.

packet A small piece of information sent over the *Internet*.

patch A short-term solution to a problem with a program, or protection against a *virus*.

pixel (picture element) A dot that is part of a picture. Everything that appears on a computer screen is made up of pixels.

platform The combination of a computer's *hardware* and the operating system it uses, such as a PC running Windows® or a Macintosh computer running the Mac operating system.

plug-in A program you can add to your *browser* to give it extra features, such as the ability to play sound or video clips.

POP (Point of Presence) A point of access to the *Internet*, usually a computer owned by an *ISP*.

POP 3 (Post Office Protocol) A system allowing you to collect your *e-mail* using any computer on the *Internet*.

portal A *Web site* that acts as a gateway to other sites.

post To send a message to a *newsgroup*.

proxy server A computer which connects a *network* such as a *LAN* to the *Internet*.

public domain Material which is not in *copyright* and can be used by anybody.

query An instruction to a *search engine* to find *Web sites* or other information.

RealAudio® A *file format* often used to play sound clips over the *Internet*.

register To give details about yourself on a *Web site* in order to receive information or software.

resolution The number of *pixels* that make up a picture. The higher the resolution, the clearer the picture.

scanner A device used to copy pictures or text from paper to a computer.

search engine A *Web site* which finds other *Web sites* or information in answer to a *query*.

secure server A computer that handles *encrypted* information, such as financial information, so that nobody else can read it.

Secure Socket Layer or **SSL** An *encryption system* built into servers and browsers that uses "identity certificates" to recognize users.

serial port The part of a computer through which data can be transmitted to a *network*.

server A computer that carries out tasks for other computers on a *network*. Some servers hold information that other computers can *download*. Others act as *links* between individual computers or small *networks* and larger ones.

shareware Software which you use free of charge for a trial period.

smiley A picture made up of keyboard characters which looks like a face.

SMTP (Simple Mail Transport Protocol) The language used to send *e-mail* via the *Internet*.

source code The *HTML* code that makes up a particular *Web page*.

spam Junk *e-mail*.

streaming A format for playing sound or video clips directly as your computer receives the data over the *Internet*.

subscribe To sign up to a *mailing list*.

surfing Exploring the *Internet*.

tag An *HTML* instruction that tells a *browser* how to display a certain part of a document.

TCP/IP (Transmission Control Protocol/ Internet Protocol) The language computers use to communicate with each other on the *Internet*.

thread A sequence of articles sent to a *newsgroup* forming a discussion on a subject.

timeout When a computer gives up trying to carry out a particular function, because it has taken too long.

trialware A basic version of a program which you use free of charge. You have to pay to use the full version.

unsubscribe To cancel a *subscription* to a *mailing list*.

upload To copy *files* from your computer to another computer via the *Internet*.

URL (Uniform Resource Locator) The unique address of a *Web page*.

Usenet The largest collection of *newsgroups* on the *Internet*.

username The name a person uses to connect to their *ISP*, which may also be the first part of their *e-mail* address.

Virtual Reality or **VR** The use of 3-D computer images to draw places and objects.

virtual world An imaginary world created using *VR*.

virus A program designed to damage other programs, *files* or computers.

WAP or **Wireless Application Protocol** A simplified version of the *Web* which can be read using devices such as mobile phones.

WAV A sound *file format* developed by Microsoft®.

Web see *World Wide Web*

Webcam A camera that can take moving pictures which can then be attached to *e-mail* or inserted in *Web* documents.

Webcast A concert or other event which is broadcast on the *Web*.

Web editor A program you can use to create *Web pages*.

Webmaster A person who creates or maintains a *Web site*.

Web page A computer document written in *HTML* and *linked* to other documents by *hyperlinks*.

Webring A group of *linked Web sites*.

Web site A collection of *Web pages* created by an organization or an individual, having the same basic *URL* and usually stored on the same computer.

Web space The space *ISPs* make available for people to create their own *Web sites*.

WinZip® A popular *compression* program.

World Wide Web or **WWW** A vast store of information available on the *Internet*. The information is produced on *Web pages* which are connected by *hyperlinks*.

WYSIWYG (What You See Is What You Get) A type of *Web editor* which shows you *Web page* content exactly as it will appear.

zipped file A *file compressed* using *WinZip*.

Useful addresses

Online services

America Online:
in the UK: **www.aol.co.uk**
For connection software call 0800 376 5432

in the US: **www.aol.com**
For connection software call 1-800 827 6364

in Canada: **www.aol.ca**
For connection software call 1-888 382 6645

in Australia: **www.aol.com.au**
For connection software call 1800 265 265

CompuServe:
in the UK: **www.compuserve.co.uk**
For connection software call 0870 600 0800

in the US: **www.compuserve.com**
For connection software call 1-800 292 3900

in Canada: **www.compuserve.ca**
For connection software call 1-888 353 8990

in Australia: **www.compuserve.com.au**
For connection software call 1300 555 520
In New Zealand call 0800 442 374

Microsoft® Network (MSN®):
in the UK: **msn.co.uk**
For connection software call 0345 202000

in the US: **msn.com**
For connection software call 1-800 373 3676

Internet Service Providers

There are hundreds of ISPs in different countries around the world. The following are just a few well-known ones. Computer magazines regularly list and review ISPs and their services – before you decide on an ISP, it's worth reading some recent magazine reviews.

In the UK:
Freeserve: **www.freeserve.com**
For connection software call 0990 500049

LineOne: **www.lineone.net**
For connection software call 0800 111210

Virgin Net: **www.virgin.net**
For connection software call 0845 650 0000

In the US:
Bluelight: **www.bluelight.com/freeinternet**
For connection software call 1-888-945-9255

Juno:**www.juno.com**
For connection software call 1-800 879 5866

Worldshare: **www.worldshare.com**
For connection software call 1-888 232 7897

In Canada:
HomeFreeWeb: **www.homefreeweb.com**
Sign up online; for customer support call 905 948 0987

Sympatico; **pre.sympatico.ca**
For connection software call 1-800 773 2121

In Australia:
One.Net: **www.one.net.au**
For connection software call 1300 550 377

OzEmail: **www.ozemail.com.au**
For connection software call 132 884

In New Zealand:
Xtra: **www.xtra.co.nz**
For connection software call 0800 22 55 98

You can find reviews of ISPs in different countries online at **www.epinions.com**

Netscape®

Netscape can act as an ISP (in the UK only), a browser (Netscape® Navigator), an e-mail program (Netscape® Messenger) and a Web editor (Netscape® Composer). Netscape in the UK is at **www.netscapeonline.co.uk**
For connection software call 0800 923 0009

Netscape in the US: **www.netscape.com**

In Canada: **www.netscape.com/en/ca**

In Australia: **www.netscape.com/au**

E-mail programs

Eudora: **www.eudora.com/email**
Eudora is available in two versions: Eudora Light is available as freeware (see page 43), or you can pay for Eudora Pro, a more advanced version.

Pegasus: **www.pegasus.usa.com**

Index

Acknowledgements

Every effort has been made to trace the copyright holders of the material in this book. If any rights have been omitted, the publishers offer their sincere apologies and will rectify this in any subsequent editions following notification.

Usborne Publishing has made every effort to ensure that material on the Web sites listed in this book is suitable for its intended purpose. However, we do not accept responsibility, and are not responsible, for any Web site other than our own. Nor will we be liable for any exposure to harmful, offensive, or inaccurate material which may appear on the Web. We recommend that children are supervised when using the Internet.

Usborne cannot guarantee that Web sites listed in this book are permanent, or that the addresses given will remain accurate, or that the information on those sites will remain as described.

Usborne Publishing will have no liability for any damage or loss caused by viruses that may be downloaded as a result of browsing the sites we recommend.

Screen shots used with permission from Microsoft Corporation. Microsoft® , Microsoft® Windows® , Microsoft® Windows® 95, Microsoft® Windows® 98, Microsoft® Outlook®, Microsoft® Outlook® Express, Microsoft® FrontPage® Express, Microsoft® Internet Explorer and Microsoft® Netmeeting® are either registered trademarks or trademarks of Microsoft Corporation in the US and other countries.

Cover   CNN/Sports Illustrated Interactive: used with permission. Maelstrom Virtual Productions Ltd.: used with permission. www.maelstrom.com Home page of the United Nations Web site: used with permission. Superscape Interactive 3D: used with permission. The Visible Human Project, US National Library of Medicine: used with permission.

p1   Globe, mouse: Digital Vision.

p2-3   OnLive! Traveler (also on p71): screen shots used with permission of Communities.com. Traveler and Talker is a trademark of Communities.com and is being used with express permission by its owner.

Space station used with permission of NASA. Virgin Net logo: used with permission. Nomad MP3 player (also on p59) used with thanks to CreativeLabs, Inc. America Online logo: ©2000 America Online, Inc. Used with permission. Palais Royal area map (also on p55): used with kind permission of RATP, Paris.

p6-7   BowieNet: ©1999 BowieNet/Ultrastar Internet Services, LLC. www.davidbowie.com Corbis Images: used with permission. www.corbis.com Starlancer game: used with permission of Digital Anvil, Inc. www.digitalanvil.com Iberia: used with permission. www.iberia.es Extract from Morgan, by Hugo Pratt, © CONG SA. www.asuivre.com/bd/prepub Untitled, by Alexander Calder, photograph © 2000 Board of Trustees, National Gallery of Art, Washington. www.nga.gov New Scientist: reproduced courtesy of newscientist.com. www.newscientist.com

TimeOut.com (also on p54): used with permission.
www.timeout.com
ViewSydney webcam: Sydney Harbour Foreshore Authority (photographer: Kim Hatton).
www.viewsydney.com.au
Virgilio: used with permission.
www.virgilio.it
Virgin Megastores online: used with permission.
www.virginmega.com
With thanks to the Washington Post **www.washingtonpost.com**.

p10-11 Modem used with thanks to 3Com, Inc.

p12-13 Freeserve, Juno and Virgin Net logos: used with permission. With thanks to Earthlink, LibertySurf, Tin.It and Wanadoo.

p14-15 America Online: ©2000 America Online, Inc. Used with permission.
CompuServe: ©2000 CompuServe Interactive Services, Inc. Used with permission.
The Microsoft Network: used with permission.

p17 Virgin Net (also on p33): used with permission.

p18-19 E-card images: Digital Vision. With thanks to Yahoo!/Claudia Baggiani.

p30 Felix is a registered trade mark. Used under agreement with the trade mark owners.

p32 Basketball, saxophone, flowers, dolphin, motorcyclist: Digital Vision. With thanks to Liszt.com.

p34 Eviaggi.com (also on p65): used with permission.
Home page of the Musée National d'Art Moderne at the Pompidou Centre, Paris: used with permission. With thanks to Barnes and Noble, El Mundo and Openbank (also on p66).

p36-37 NASA and the Galileo Project: used with permission. With thanks to BBC Online and the Tate Gallery, London.

p39 *Portrait of Pierre Quthe*, François Clouet (c.1522-1572), photo © RMN/J.G. Berizzi.
Bouquet of Flowers in an Arch, Ambrosius Bosschaert (1573-1621), photo © RMN/C. Jean
Self-portrait, Albrecht Dürer (1471-1528), photo © RMN/Arnaudet
The Tree of Crows, Caspar David Friedrich (1774-1840), photo © RMN/Arnaudet.

p40-41 MyCitySites – London: Less Rain. MyCitySites – Barcelona: Vasava Artworks, SL.
With thanks to the Royal Academy, London.

p44-45 Yahoo! and Yahoo! UK and Ireland screen shots: ©1994-2000 Yahoo! Inc. All rights reserved. With thanks to Caixa de Catalunya and Discovery Channel.

p46-47 AltaVista: ©2000 AltaVista Company. All rights reserved.

p48-49 Copernic: used with permission.
Metacrawler: used with permission of Go2Net, Inc. All rights reserved.
Map of Georgia and monuments used with thanks to the Parliament of the Republic of Georgia.
With thanks to Ask Jeeves! and National Geographic.

p50-51 Benetton F1 and Sportal: used with permission of Sportal.com. With thanks to BBC Online and ZD Net.

p52-53 Babelfish: ©2000 AltaVista Company. All rights reserved.
CNN Interactive: used with permission.
Le Monde: used with permission.
With thanks to AFP, Encyclopaedia Britannica, The Guardian Unlimited Lenta, The New York Times, Quid and La Stampa.

p54-55 Moviefone: ©2000 America Online, Inc. Used with permission.
Railtrack: courtesy of Railtrack plc.
Paris metro map used with kind permission of RATP, Paris.
With thanks to Alitalia.

p56-57 Imperial War Museum: courtesy of the Imperial War Museum.
Museum of Modern Art, New York: used with permission.
National Gallery, London: used with permission.
Rijksmuseum – page design: Eden Design & Communication. ©2000 Rijksmuseum, Amsterdam.
With thanks to the American Museum of Natural History, Château de Versailles, the Metropolitan Museum, New York, Musée national d'histoire naturelle, Paris and the Musée d'Orsay, Paris.

p58-59 With thanks to Harmony Central, NME, Sony Music Ltd. and The Ultimate Band List.

p60-61 CNN/Sports Illustrated Interactive: used with permission.
Complete Snowboarder: ©2000 Complete Travel Ltd.
With thanks to the Bundesliga, Chelsea Football Club, FC Barcelona, Juventus, Skicentral and Sports.com.

p62-63 Background (also p64-65, 66-67, 76-77): Digital Vision.
AudioStreet: Streets Online Limited. Used with permission.
BoxMan: ©1997-2000 Boxman.com plc.
Haburi: used with permission.
With thanks to Bol.com.

p64-65 Food.com: courtesy of Food.com.
Lastminute.com: used with permission.
With thanks to E-bookers, Interflora, RedGift.com, Sainsbury's and Travelocity.

p66-67 EasyDiary: used with permission.

eCash: eCash Technologies, Inc. Used with permission.
The Hunger Site: used with permission.
p66-67 (cont/d) The Motley Fool: used with permission.
With thanks to Beenz, Médecins Sans Frontières and TheStreet.com.

p68-69   Backgammon from pogo.com: used with permission.
Majesty ©2000 Hasbro Interactive Inc. All rights reserved. ©2000 Cyberlore Studios Inc. All rights reserved. Published by Hasbro Interactive Inc. Developed by Cyberlore Studios Inc.
Screen shots of Real Pool and Shockwave Foosball reproduced with permission of shockwave.com.

p70   Space shuttle and space station used with permission of NASA.
Girl wearing VR headset: Digital Vision.

p71 Turtle images: © The Natural History Museum, London.
OnLive! Traveler: screen shots with permission of Communities.com.
Traveler and Talker is a trademark of Communities.com and is being used with express permission by its owner.

p72-73   Yahoo! UK and Ireland screen shots: ©1994-2000 Yahoo! Inc. All rights reserved.
Excite screen display: ©2000 Excite UK Ltd.
Internet cafe: Cyberia, Paris ©Frederick Froument

p74-75   mIRC screen shot: ©1995-2000 Tjerk Vonck & mIRC Co. Ltd.

mIRC® is a registered trademark of mIRC Co Ltd.
Dobedo screen shot and icons: © Dobedo 2000. Used with permission.

WebPhone®: © NetSpeak Corporation 1995-2000. All Rights Reserved. NetSpeak, the NetSpeak logo and WebPhone are registered trademarks of NetSpeak Corporation.

P77   Elvis: Pictorial Press Ltd
www.pictorialpress.co.uk
Motorcyclist, trumpeter, lizard, dice, keyboard and mouse, hot air balloon, footballer, satellite, rosette: Digital Vision.

p81   Macromedia® Dreamweaver®: used with permission.

p83   Tiger, dancers, motorcyclists, swimmer: Digital Vision.

p87   Trumpets, dolphins, soccer player and ball: Digital Vision.

p90   With thanks to the US Navy.

p91   NASA: used with permission.
Florida Museum of Natural History: used with permission.

p95   Museum of Science and Industry, Chicago. Copyright © Museum of Science and Industry, Chicago, USA.

p96-97   Windsurfer: Digital Vision.
Group 42: used with permission.

p98   Aquarium du Québec: used with permission.

Aquarium de San Sebastián: used with permission.
Minnesota Aquarium: used with permission.

p100   Sound card, speakers and microphone used with thanks to CreativeLabs, Inc.

p102-103   Hand animation © Webpromotion, Inc.
Java and all Java-based trademarks and logos are trademarks or registered trademarks of Sun Microsystems, Inc. in the United States and other countries.
Java planets used with thanks to WebTamers.
Reversi game: used with permission of Hridayesh K Gupta.

p106   Netserver Storage System/6: used with permission of Hewlett Packard.

p108-109   WS_FTP: © Ipswitch, Inc., used with permission.

p110-111   Cable modem: Motorola CyberSURFR™ , used with permission of Motorola.
Cables: Image Bank/Lars Ternblad.
Soccer match: Ben Radford/Allsport.
With thanks to Citroën SA, Sony Corporation and Sun Microsystems.

p112-113   Cassiopeia Pocket PC, used with permission of Casio, Inc.
Psion Revo, used with permission of Psion UK Ltd.
With thanks to Nokia and Samsung.

117   Net Nanny: used with permission